YOU ARE MY QUEST

YOU ARE
MY
QUEST

A MEDIEVAL TALE

JORGE LUIS GONZALEZ-ROMO

You are my Quest
A Medieval Tale

© Jorge Luis Gomzalez-Romo

Edition: JAOTL
Cover and layout design:
Brenda Vázquez Pedroza

Printed in México

First edition: March 2019

ISBN: 978-0-578-48754-0

To Patricia;

Heed of a tale from days of yore;
when good and evil were more simply defined.
when evil was not concentrated and spread wide
there was no black and white.
Back when love was not a fairy tale.

Before this story is told,
first allow me to set the tone,
so that there is no need
to escape the troubles of the modern world,
for together we shall venture,
and recall the elements of fairy tales.

CONTENTS

Chapter I 1
Chapter II 14
Chapter III 17
Chapter IV 25
Chapter V 32
Chapter VI 35
Chapter VII 41
Chapter VIII 57
Chapter IX 60
Chapter X 67
Chapter XI 72
Chapter XII 83
Chapter XIII 89
Chapter XIV 97
Chapter XV 100
Chapter XVI 112

CHAPTER I

ॐॐॐ

T he keep has been breached, it is over!" said queen Riko, giving voice to defeat. His trusted samurai, Junichi, replied: "I swore to protect you! Your highness, heed me well; buildings are not important. You will live. I shall protect you, and the people will follow you, my queen." The general of the royal guard, the best swordsman in the land spoke, uttering voice to determination.

"It is not the palace I speak of, but rather the walls that protect my hollow heart," she said, and general Junichi stopped, yet his warriors kept barricading the main entrance.

I profess my feelings
you hide behind selfless duty.
A war on two fronts.

She continued, "I can see it in your eyes as we are about to die. Look at me and do not tell me you do not feel the same impulse as I!"

"I can not protect your highness, if I am focused in such a way," said the gallant general, moving to aid his fellow soldiers. For his valor denied any drive of action that intended to taint him in stains of defeat. To this he uttered words of courage, "Once the enemy comes forth, what shall they face?"

In unity the royal guard, only fifty left, shouted, "Our mighty blades!" The enemies outside heard the battle cry, and the last word that echoed resonated fear, "FUA!" – a phrase that is simply defined as the drive that lifts the spirit when the mind and body say no.

The queen rushed to the general's side saying: "When will you stop hiding behind your honor?" He did not reply. To him the enemy outside was not as dangerous as the feelings she offered. This distraction would make him lose focus.

Thinking of you now.
I wish you'd open up to me
but you are fighting.

"I would rather commit seppuku by piercing my heart than live another everlasting minute in fear that either of us shall perish without first having our hearts speak their truths!" She said while her general saw her drawing out her knife to take her life. The samurai rescued her, saying: "Do not be a coward. I saved you, as it is my duty, but a general, a soldier, can not love his queen!"

"If I can not force you to love me, I will command your men to kill themselves so that their honor is preserved!"

"Do not force my mind to engage in a war on two fronts!" He matched his voice with hers. "I trained your army to not fear shame. We are determined to die in battle, rather than commit suicide!"

"Junichi, there is no future. Even if we survive, for you alone can wipe out our foes with your skills, I cannot live this way." She lowered her voice and in tears ended, "Not anymore."

A soldier approached them saying, "My queen, my general, the enemy will soon enter. Please save yourselves, escape and live in the countryside far from…" an arrow pierced his throat, the enemy was inside the main hall. Junichi grabbed Riko and together, the two lovers retreated as Junichi slew any who crossed his path. Finally they hid in the bathhouse while the royal guard defended their mistress. Junichi held his attention to the enemy, his right hand holding his blade, his left protecting his only love.

Samurai of my heart
I demand: Lay down your soul!
Your sword or soul-mate?

"Junichi, please look at me. I offer you an alternative." He turned, allowing her into his heart. "Embrace me, take a deep breath along with me, and let us fall, to wash our agony. Only if you are determined to save me, give me your breath as you unite your lips with mine. I say this not as your queen, for if you carry out my petition you will leave behind your blade. We shall embrace and either live with our breath, drown together, or die by a Shogun who forbade this love."

Junichi found in his eyes a new purpose by hearing the words of his queen. Unstrapping his katana—a blade that represented his soul, the fighting determination that pledged to serve his queen—threw it across the room. "I lay down my sword to raise my arms so to love you." He embraced Riko, kissed her, and said, "Take a deep breath, for it might be our last." The samurai held her close as they fell into the pool.

In the shallow deep water, with closed eyes the lovers exchanged a cycle of air. The serene atmosphere of the bathhouse, provided by the general and the queen, as they were both willing to give their lives to their forbidden love was interrupted when Junichi felt a grip pulling him out of the water.

Gasping for air and regaining his senses, looking around to recall events to his memory, Junichi saw his queen was motionless—face down in the water like a dead fish. In that moment he uttered a cry of sorrow. Junichi tried to break free from his captor's embrace, but was not strong enough; his lungs had no air to provide energy to his muscles.

One man was not enough to drag the defeated general out of the water. It was as if his will pinned him to the floor, commanding his mind to rush and save his queen. The more the Shogun's soldiers tried to carry him, the less he budged. His right hand seeking to hold Riko one last time, only a few inches away.

"Someone pull her out of the water!" Junichi shouted hysterically and in pain. There were three soldiers who intended to pull the general, when another rushed inside the pool and lifted the queen. Junichi shouted and struggled to aid her when her body moved like a rag doll. He lowered his body, seeking her out, and cried in lament.

More soldiers entered the room, still trying to move the resilient warrior, but they did not manage to move him out of the water. The commotion and voice of lament ended when the general was knocked unconscious with the butt of a spear. The force dropped him back along with three other soldiers into the pool.

"Chain him and bring him before the Shogun while he is motionless," said the one who dealt the silencing blow. They managed to carry him out of the water while his body was flat on the ground, as the soldiers began to wrap his hands the general mumbled, "Riko, it was my life that should have been taken. I failed you." Junichi lifted his head to take one last look. The soldier holding the spear knelt and said, "this is a hard dog to kill. If only our men where like him," and punched the general in the face.

When general Junichi regained consciousness he was in the presence of the Shogun. They were in the throne room, still in ruins from the battle. The Shogun siting in the throne, his men in two separate rows, and the general in the middle only appeared as ornaments that were not disrupted by the battle while the furniture was completely destroyed. The walls held arrows and the windows and blinds were tainted with blood.

"It is good that you are finally awake," said the Shogun. There was a long pause. The new lord of all Japan said calmly, "Someone release his restraints. Allow the general to be more comfortable." As a man approached to cut his binds, Junichi did not reply. His visage was calm. The sorrow had vanished and there was no sting of anger. He simply took serene breaths. His yellow eyes stared deep into the Shogun. Rarely blinking, as if a duel that the general denied to lose.

"Impudent dog!" shouted one of the Shogun's soldiers, standing to the left flank. "Your new lord will not wait until you find your tongue!"

"I have not expressed thus," said the Shogun lifting a hand and signaling the soldier to stand down. Still his glance did not leave the general's. The Shogun lost contact when a soldier entered and whispered to his lord. In turn, he replied to the messenger so only he could hear, who afterwards bowed and left the room.

"I have been informed that your queen is dead," said the Shogun. To his surprise Junichi did not react, rather he remained as he was, followed by a long pause. The Shogun continued: "Your army has been defeated and your purpose as a samurai is no more. What have you to say?"

Junichi blinked but did not speak. His eyes sought to listen, waiting to see what lie in store for him. Deep down he was shattered. His duty, his whole life, was to protect the queen and he had failed. Therefore he knew there was no worse fate than this.

"As a merciful lord, seeing how you fought with bravery, I will allow you, General Junichi, to commit seppuku so that your tittle and honor may be preserved after you die. I will make sure your heroic deeds are perpetuated in the records of history, and that songs and poetry be written in your name."

Junichi smiled, lifting his cheek. Finally the samurai replied with no shame in his voice: "so long as I am alive I can regain my honor. Defeat brings me no shame, and if you think I want to escape with an act of cowardice such as suicide, then you are mistaken."

"Henceforth, I forbid you to seek revenge. Furthermore, you are banished forthwith under punishment of death." Junichi did not alter his expression, there was no shock, and he was not surprised. With a small grin the Shogun said, "Not only are you a ronin—a master-less samurai without a queen, but a heartless man with no one to serve."

By hearing those last words Junichi's face turned to gloom. The path that lay ahead, living under the sadness of his loss became clear. His duty as a samurai was lost, and even if he tried to conceal his feelings with dignity, the reality of being a heartless man was the true woe, dejected from any moment of being with his beloved Riko. Alas in life, in service to the queen, his heart was at ease. Now he had to face being alone. Junichi's eyes looked at the floor. He may not take his own life, but he did feel in the company of death for Riko, his one and only love was no more.

"Will my lord allow me a final statement?" Asked the defeated general, finding the eyes of the Shogun once more, whom answered: "Be brief."

"It is true that I loved the queen, yet my affection was no different than the dedication a samurai has towards the lord he serves. My devotion was to her and to preserve her honor, valuing it above my own. I can live with no shame because I did my duty even though I wish I had died for her. Now I am here and this gladdens me as I will pay a bigger price of shame, for had she been alive, her fate would not have been gentle. I welcome my punishment."

"Junichi," said the shogun with a pause, expressing frustration, "It is time for you to leave. If you have not left my borders by three days, you will be hunted down."

Junichi stood up and began to walk towards the self-imposed ruler of Japan and said: "Live with the knowledge that it was the gossip of the queen's forbidden love and your ambition to become Shogun that killed your daughter." The Shogun's face heated up with anger. He exploded saying: "Get this thing out of my sight!"

Two soldiers approached from either side to escort Junichi outside. He rejected being dragged by them, with a swift move he grabbed the wrist of one soldier and forced him to the ground. Blades, spears, and all attention turned to Junichi who let him go without harm and said: "I can find my own way."

Once the Shogun observed the ronin walking on the road from a window in the throne room overlooking the region, he addressed the messenger who gave him the news of the queen moments earlier: "You say Riko is alive?"

"Yes my lord, however it is as if she were dead, she has not spoken since she woke up," said the messenger.

"Take me to her at once!"

The messenger led the Shogun to a lonely room where Riko stood motionless, only staring into empty space. The Shogun adopted the persona of her father and tried to get her attention, yet she did not seem to notice a thing around her. The Shogun leaned down and whispered into her ear, "I have grave news: your faithful samurai is dead. Once he was surrounded he pierced his neck with a piece of wood. The coward did not try to defend you. Do know that you will be properly attended and looked after, dear daughter?" She did not weep nor react to the news. Even as the Shogun rose and closed the door to her room, Riko remained quiet. A life without her beloved samurai was no life. All she wanted was to be with him, but now life turned pale, it was meaningless. There was no reason to cry or to lament. She simply closed her eyes, wishing that she could have been a peasant, for her life to have meaning.

When the self-appointed lord returned to his throne, he gave a sigh of relief, laughing at his plan. "So long as Junichi thinks Riko is dead, there is no one to oppose me!"

It took the once proud samurai, now a wandering ronin, six days to walk from Osaka to Nagasaki in hope of taking a one-way trip to Europe. The Dutch were the only foreign nation allowed to trade with Japan. In the event that there was no ship, he had to sail to China or India. News of Junichi's exile traveled fast. When he stopped for food or rest the people were kind to him. In six days the land began to feel the gloom of the queen's absence. Queen Riko had been a rightful ruler who looked after the people, but the Shogun set in motion a civil war by assassinating clan leaders, in the hope of conquering those who opposed him and other samurai like Junichi, who defended the people, were no more.

"Take the fight to the Shogun, the people support your samurai code. Preserve what the queen gave us," said the owner of the inn in Hirado.

"I am a peasant and no longer a warrior. The code of the samurai does not apply to a wanderer. If I seek revenge I will plague the whole kingdom and condemn innocent lives. My duty to the land is over," replied the ronin.

The innkeeper did not believe that noble people had to bow to rulers such as the Shogun. Junichi stood up and asked a soldier who, like himself, was resting from his duty and drinking sake, "What is your name?"

"It is Nobuo," he instantly stood up and bowed.

"You need not to bow before me, I am no longer a samurai." Junichi lifted him up. "If tomorrow I do not leave, you have to carry out my execution as commanded by the Shogun. But I beg you, with your authority, negotiate with the Dutch so that I may sail far away."

Looking at the cracks in the floor before bowing to acknowledge his orders the man replied, "I will do as you say, but Japan without a samurai such as you is no Japan." Nobuo was determined to keep Junichi safe, but expressed his concern with worry in his voice.

By noon of the next day the Dutch vessel arrived in Hirado. The procedure to inspect the cargo was immediately carried out. The crew, along with Japanese soldiers, began to unload the vessel. Meanwhile the captain stood next to Nobuo. From a corner Junichi overlooked the procedure and was surprised by the uncomfortable silence that surrounded both the captain and Nobuo. An hour passed by and Junichi approached the inspection scene and whispered in Japanese to his brother-in-arms, saying: "Excuse me, Nobuo-san is there something you can ask the captain on my behalf?" But he only turned and looked nervous.

Junichi exhaled, shaking his head in disbelief and addressed the Dutch man directly, "Captain, allow me the distinguished honor of meting you, I am a humble traveler by the name of Junichi," he said, bowing as low as his back allowed him and once he stood straight he extended his right hand in order to shake the captain's hand with a western greeting.

"The honor is mine sir," the captain instantly accepted the greeting shaking Junichi's hand. "I am captain Theunis of the vessel Beyla, at your service."

"I thank you captain, but allow me to be at your service on your ship, in exchange for passage to Europe. As a poet, I wish to explore and enrich my knowledge outside of Japan."

The expression of the captain was that of surprise, with a nod he replied, "In all my voyages to this distinguished land, I have never meet a Japanese man eager to leave. Trade may easily enter Japan so long as it is not restricted, but exportation is out of the question. Even if I willingly let you on board, customs will not allow it."

"I fully understand captain, I do not seek to complicate your trade. More so, when the person in charge of your inspection is next to you." Junichi finished by looking at Nobuo, indirectly signaling him to vouch on his behalf.

"If this man wants to venture outside of Japan," Nobuo replied nervously with a pause, "I have no problem whatsoever."

The captain smiled at Nobuo in surprise, then added, "I do not have to speak Japanese in order to hear worry in your voice. What about the documentation? I certainly do not want to lose my trading privileges due to smuggling!" The captain exploded, making his intentions clear His reaction made Nobuo even more nervous.

"You!" a solider shouted.

Instantly all eyes turned to search for who was being addressed. "You!" shouted the voice again, coming from a patrol guard in company of five fully armed soldiers who approached Junichi, surrounding him. "I know you," said the same patrolman addressing the lone wanderer. "You are the ronin the Shogun has placed a price on."

"Go ahead, delay my trip!" shouted captain Theunis as he stepped aside when a soldier signaled for him to move. When he was in the corner with his hands crossed and his left foot on the wall, he continued, "Hopefully I will get to see a crazy show. I hear samurai can end a duel with a single blow."

During the commotion Junichi did not move nor move his eyes from the patrolman who questioned him. If this was the end of the journey, Junichi was ready to accept his fate but held his ground.

"Why are you so eager to leave?" asked the patrolman.

"I am a humble poet, and I only seek to enrich my eyes with other beauteous sights than that of Japan," Junichi said in a calm tone.

The patrolman smiled, taking two steps back saying, "Let's hear a poem then!"

The ronin looked to his right, then slowly glanced to his left. He was completely surrounded. Junichi closed his eyes, pressed his lips together, exhaled, and whispered to himself, "No mind." Clearing his throat, he began to recite:

"The Maid at the Bay

A maid by the seashore
looking at the horizon from afar,
awaiting a sailor who is gone.
Time must be bizarre.

For she owns a melancholic look,
like sadness, filled with sorrow,
I must be reading her like a book
taking me to mount Kilimanjaro.

She loves a loving hate;
her choice is now regret.
Reaching a cognitive state
forever to be upset.

Like the clouds that are grey,
she now fades away."

Suddenly there was silence in the port. Only the melody of the birds was heard. Moments later a soldier said, "That was beautiful." The patrolman who asked for the poem looked meditative and added, "This reminds me of someone I left in Okinawa many years ago."

"I could swear it sounded like a broken sonnet, no form but the content and delivery amazing," said captain Theunis.

"It is clear you are not the ronin we are looking for," said the patrolman to the poet, then addressed the Dutch captain saying, "I see no problem with allowing one of our countrymen to leave so that one day we can be enriched by his findings. Let me apologize for delaying you captain, in return I shall worry about any further paperwork, I will make sure to speed up the process." The patrolman made a signal and within three minutes the vessel was ready to leave.

Junichi looked at the life he was leaving behind. To his surprise, there was nothing to miss. Before stepping onboard, Nobuo approached him, "I was afraid the patrol was going to execute you, please forgive me, I was not brave enough to carry out your favor."

"There is nothing to forgive Nobuo-san," Junichi placed his right palm on his shoulder, "Do remember that gentle words are mightier than the sword, even if the blade is as beautiful and honorable as the Katana."

The ronin who crossed Japan concealed his inner thoughts and began to sail away onboard the Beyla, determined to leave Japan, and his life as a warrior, in the past. Junichi, as a poet, contemplated the image of departing with the sunset and the realization to never see the land of the Rising Sun again, and said:

"Japan wrote their poems in leaves.
In this welcoming night,
the crescent shadow of the moon
caresses my spirit like a blossom.

The cuckoo cries before dawn
and I hope to hear you snore."

"What is that you now recited?" asked the captain, approaching Junichi.

"I recited a poem inspired from the Man'yoshu," said Junichi, finding the captain standing next to him, and then returned his gaze to the setting sun.

"A bit long and too many syllables, don't you think?" criticized the Captain.

"Five, seven then five
syllables mark a haiku
not what I just said."

There was a pause as captain Theunis contemplated the play of words. With the last glimmer of twilight Junichi turned around to face the captain explaining, "Haiku are not the only form of poems in Japan. The first ever recorded are said to be 100 leaves."

"By the way you contemplate the sunset and recite poetry, I dare say you are trying to be someone you are not."

"I am leaving a life behind," said Junichi, now gazing the final moments of twilight. Then darkness covered his homeland with shadows of tyranny from the self-imposed Shogun who stripped him of his duty.

"You really are the one those patrolmen were looking for," said the captain moments later. Junichi calmly responded, "Like I said, I am a humble poet."

"Frankly, I do not care. Is not like I am going to turn you in, I do not wish to be delayed." Captain Theunis paused then continued, "There is a phrase that states: 'those who live by the sword, will perish and meet the same fate.' You might not have drawn a blade, but your new weapon is more honorable." With those final words, the captain gently bowed before his guest.

"I thank you captain, but poetry and words are not a weapon. I am leaving my old life behind yet I cannot deny the part of me that is samurai. I long to serve. In the time while we arrive to Europe I am at your service, please assign me any task," he said, returning the bow.

"Junichi, you are the most distinguished Japanese man I have met. You will help me plot charts and look at the sky to navigate so that it feeds your poetic sight."

"Thank you, captain, so let us get started!"

CHAPTER II

Once upon a time...

There are castles
made of sand,
there are castles made of gold
and dreams that transport you
to distant lands.

The dragon soaring in the sky,
blazing its red flame of light
leaving no trace behind.

The white unicorn as it rides
on endless green fields
through the pines of the forest
as the wind blows still,
catching your doubts.

Once upon a time
awake those dreams of old.

Tick, tock - the clock
counts down the hour hand
of a special day
yet to unfold.

No, no—that is not the way to start. You will think this is a fairy tale, but surely it is not. There are elements of a fairy tale: it has brave warriors who hold their values, such as samurai Junichi, and his journey has not reached its end. There are beautiful princess from far of lands, magic and true love, ending with a happy ever after.

Although history and reality portray that love is not ordinary, it is an unexceptional hardship. Those who find love, make others dull in its pursuit. Life can change in a matter of seconds—like the sands of time, life follows a straight path. There is no going back for one does not step in the same river twice. One moment you can feel loved, another you can feel hated. Everything you see is in the past, never to be reckoned with again because we live in the present. A choice can be altered by a second. A whole life changed by love.

What may be thy choice?
For it is life
that will change
by one choice.
What is thou feeleth
Sprung from precious thought
overcometh by desire
that moves thee in restless pursuit
so to fulfill that goal,
from which all thy life has meaning?

In the matters of the heart it is left to the choice of two:
Two that may be brought together.
Two that may perish and lose.
Two choices,

Two people,
Two lives.
In the flow of time
Two lives can change
by the feelings of love.

Love is manifested in many ways. Butterflies swirl around the mind, making the stomach grumble. The mind spins and that one person occupies all, and every thought. Oh time, desires you to remain at their side. Songs lose their lyrics only to whisper in your ear their name, feeding the heart. Culminating in dreams, prayers, and wishful thinking to wait patiently for the day to be at their side. Do not cry dear reader for you are at my side. "Who am I?" you question, well it seems that introducing myself is a good place to start this story.

CHAPTER III

❧ ❦

O nce upon a time there was a miller by the name of John who had three workers: Jack, Jim, and Yrian, yours truly. My name originates from medieval Scandinavia. With my humble disposition to my work, I was the most honored of the three. While I carried out all the duties, Jack and Jim rested, taking advantage of my good nature. Often times they asked me to do their chores too, which I gladly accepted.

I lifted heavy sacks of flour while my fellow mates played games and even waged their week's earnings in cards. "Yrian, you do not mind taking this barrel to old John, do you?" Jack, the fatter one said.

"Not at all, Jack," was my attitude.

"That is a good lad," Jim, the shortest, replied with a coy smile on his cheeks as the two witnessed how easy it was to get away from their daily obligations. They laughed at me for lifting a barrel when I had the option to push it, but I wanted to get stronger.

John approached us saying, "Gentlemen I need my clock to be fixed, we need supplies to repair the mill's spinning water wheel, and pay the bills. Taxes are upon us. Now you can divide those three tasks among yourselves, but I need them done," then he vanished.

"Hey Yrian, would you mind going to town and running those errands?" said Jack.

"We have to look after the mill and there is much to be done here," Jim added.

"Good point you guys, I think I can be back in an hour."

"No need to rush, take your time," the two answered in unison. Once I was on the road towards town, I noticed them taking cover in shade of the big tree in front of the mill. Surely, they were overwhelmed by their hard work. Without jealousy, I set out towards the town. The mill where I worked was located by the river twenty minutes away from town.

My first stop was the clock shop. As I opened the door there were clocks of all sorts hanging from the ceiling, and the tables had other varieties. As I made my way towards the counter there was a rhythmical voice saying:

"In the beginning
there was the void. Emptiness
surrounded by chaos.

Before there was a
start to all, there was nothing.
Time marks completion.

Time is motion and
displacement. A life span is
ticking like a clock."

The clock master was waltzing from section to section. When he began to hum, I interrupted, "Excuse me good sir, can I have a moment?" He stopped and approached me, but continued, as I stood motionless and confused.

"I see you hide from
my gaze, looking at your side—
an hour has gone by.

Thinking of you now
I wish to see you blossom
but you are away"

"I do not understand, I am here in your presence." The man
avoided my question and exclaimed full of joy and with concern for
nothing more, but this time he stopped using the rhythmical voice.
"In this very moment you are, but who is to say a moment later? I
was reciting odes for Time—my superior." He gestured, pointing
towards a big clock.

"I will like a word with the person in charge, if you please," I said,
still confused.

"Indeed, I apologize, where are my manners? I am Timothy, the
owner of Tick-Tock Shop, but the master, and the one whom we are
all accountable is Time." There was a pause, then Timothy asked,
"You know what time is, right?"

I was about to answer his question, rather say the first thing that
came to mind, but he interrupted me, "Of course you do not! No
one can explain time!"

"It appears that you do," said an elderly voice from a corner.

"The Time Wizard has spoken!" exclaimed Timothy, turning
around to face him in haste. As the elder began to slowly approach
us, there was silence and no more ramblings from Timothy. When
he was in front of me, he asked, "How can I be of service?"

"Please, can this pocket watch be fixed?" I presented the ob-
ject. The old man took it gently, then without taking his eyes from
mine, he extended his right hand in the direction of Timothy, saying, "Make yourself useful and do not," he paused, then lowering
his tone and facing young Timothy concluded, "do not waste this
young man's time with your ramblings." He went to the back room

and the old man followed him with his eyes. When Timothy was gone the old man exhaled saying, "Please forgive my son. He is jovial that I retired and gave him full ownership of the store while I simply supervise."

No sooner did the elder finish, when Timothy came out, "Here it is, good as new!" The elder took it, examined the pocket watch closely, then put it next to his ear. With a smile he said, "Yes, it stands in perfect condition," then presented the watch back to me.

"Dad, tell our guest how you invented the clock."

"No, you mindless fool!" The elder turned and confronted his son, "This young man has duties to attend, unlike you!"

"I do not mind, but I do have a question; why sell clocks?"

There was no further arguing, both turned to face me. "Well, clocks…" the old man was about to answer until Timothy stepped in, using his rhythmical tone again.

"Clocks track the motion of time, while church bells chime, signaling the day ticking by. The only crime, like vapor, is to sublime to a new phase. In essence to the flowing river with currents and tides, mime the undulating path that may never be tamed."

The elder looked at his son saying, "Since you tell the story better, recite for us, just be brief." He calmly pulled out two chairs. He placed the chair in such a way so his back faced the wall and rested his arm on the support of the chair. I sat mesmerized by what Timothy was about to say.

"There once was: a wheel, an arrow, and a grain of sand, whom were entrusted the task of organizing events, while keeping track of their surroundings. Each was given the freedom of creativity. The one who stood apart would hence become time.

'The wheel decided that with every spin, images in a turning motion to be captured and stored behind its trail. The arrow simply began to move in one direction, with no further care of stopping, while sand was oblivious. To the grain of sand, completing the task seemed distant. Uncertainty surrounded its mind, leaving upcoming events unknown. Undisturbed by the objects' reaction, the Grand

Master approached them in a serene mood." Timothy made a reverent gesture towards his father who lifted his eyes up, shaking his head in disbelief, not accepting the praise.

"Gently, the Master strung a bow and shot the arrow inside the wheel which began to spin, moving with the constant inertia of the arrow. Eventually, the wheel became weary of motion and stopped. The arrow, however, kept moving but the wheel became motionless. Each interval of the arrow, by the second, produced a beating sound. With every echo passing by, the Grand Master felt that each period and every re-vibration was a new phase. But why did you not touch the sand, wise master?" Timothy concluded, extending both arms towards his father.

Timothy's father then said, "The Grand Master left sand untouched because he knew deep within that even as each moment moved from now to the next, there was doubt. Applauding the disposition of sand, the Grand Master acknowledged that the future could not be changed. Thus, given the freedom to decide, a clock helps the individual to be responsible and keep track of the day."

"That is the nature of time and why we work at Tick-Tock shop," Timothy concluded.

"Hearing that story and being inside this shop makes me appreciate time even more. Which I deeply thank you but I must be going, I still have other duties to attend," I said.

Timothy's father stood up, moved the chair aside and added, "Of course you do, time is of the essence after all, and working with old John is no easy task." My face then became more confused. "This is a small town lad, but few acknowledge your honest work. Let me walk you out."

Once outside, I had the sensation that a long time had passed, "How long did I wait in your shop?"

"For people who are always in a hurry, and take a brief moment to relax, the experience is a bit unusual. All you have to remember is:

The waking dawn brings
a new day forth
as a beam of light
renews your spirit.

Out of fear
do not worry
on the coming future.
Murky paths are
clouded by time.

Oh why does it go by fast?
What if I could own every second?

No need to complain nor ponder.
Acknowledge from within;
to allow time move
along its stopples path."

The old man paused, "If you remember the meaning behind the 'Wheel of Time,' you will see that each moment will be unique."

"I thank you for your lesson, now can I ask for your name?"

The old man stood straight and with a playful smile answered, "Really, you heard the rhymes of my son, observed my shop, and even listened to a story about it and yet, you ask?" The old man exhaled with a laugh. "It's fine. I can't blame you, for no one can really explain time in simple terms."

"You are time?" Not only did I find it hard to utter, but also found it hard to believe.

"That is how my name is pronounced, but it is written. T-Y-M-E, but call me old Tim if you wish. Anyway, I am glad you stopped by and took a moment to hear my son's ramblings, do send my regards to John. Best of wishes on your errands, lad." Having said that and shaking my hand, Old Tim went back inside his shop.

The rest of my chores went by faster, and to my surprise, when I returned John summoned me the moment he saw me saying, "I am glad you came back in less than an hour Yrian, we really have to fix the mill. Tomorrow I have to make a delivery," he shouted across the field when I came into view. In haste, I sprinted to work on the maintenance of the spare parts. With hard work, the mill was fully functional before dusk.

Night struck, the day of labor ended, and the four of us sat to have dinner. John took a moment to express his future plans. Normally, he started with his long-term goals, followed by a plan of action starting with the next day. This was not anything unusual for the end of each month, but this night was different.

"Lads, soon I will retire and I plan to spend the rest of my days resting. Boy do I deserve it; I have been working since I can remember, heaven's sake! I can't recall when I last had a vacation. This implies that I do not wish to work, nor have anything to do with this mill. Being that it is a fair source of income, it is time for a new owner. And what better owner than one who knows the labors of this mill just as well as I do, and that should be one of you! I say this to the three of you, because each one of you has been working the same amount of time, and I want to be as fair as possible. The decision to pass down the mill will not be determined by how long or how hard you have worked, but by other means. I will entitle the mill to whoever brings me the finest horse. It is really that simple! After all, I need means of transportation if I am going to travel and I need to do so in style! Hey, it's fair right? I've given you work and experience in the know-how of not just the mill but also in other areas, now you are about to do something in return for me and there is greatness ahead for the three of you, no doubt, despite who becomes the owner. Best of wishes and may the best man win!" John stood up, and concluded by offering us a safe journey.

"Jack, Jim, what are your thoughts on the matter?" I asked moments later.

"It sounds like we don't have to work tomorrow," said Jack.

"Yeah why not wake up by late afternoon and sleep in?" Jim responded.

"Have a decent lunch and head out to visit the wealthiest ranches of the region," added Jack.

Jim then asked me with a mouth full of his diner, "What about you Yrian?" I'm not sure if he was curious about the competition, but at the time that did not matter much to me.

"I am thinking of waking up before dawn, walking in the direction of the forest, greeting the sunrise, and reaching the landlord's kingdom."

"You will travel off the main road?" Jack replied in surprise, spitting out his drink.

"In the middle of nowhere? Well, good luck finding a horse," Jim finally said.

I did not bother with their comments; I simply went to sleep and woke up before dawn.

CHAPTER IV

ᡈ᠎᠎ᡈ

I was renewed when the rays of the sun greeted me, hearing the song of the birds, I was energized by each step, and watched the squirrels as they jumped from tree to tree with the heartiness of the forest vigor within me. I passed a green frog and bowed down to say hello, removing my orange hat. Before crossing the river, I glanced over as the fish jumped around the waterfall. Then, making use of a log that connected both ends of the river, I crossed like a circus acrobat. I never felt lost the day, but after dusk my feet were tired and so I had to rest underneath the moon's light.

"Good morning," greeted an old, wrinkly voice. When I fully awoke and opened my eyes there was an old lady before me. She then asked, "What are you doing deep inside the forest?"

"Well," I yawned shaking away the fatigue, "it so happens I seek the landlord in order to acquire the most majestic horse, I will then offer it to my craft master, John the Miller."

The old lady did not nod, she simply said, "Will you help an old person like me to gather some wood?"

"Surely, madam!" I did not hesitate to reply nor question that by helping her I was being distracted from my task. With my best disposition, I collected all the wood and carried it over to the hut of the mysterious lady. Once I laid down the wood, I immediately noticed there were details to attend to. First, I fixed the celling of her hut so to prevent leaks in the event of rain. Next, I took two buckets to the river and filled them with water. Along the way, I gathered some fruit and placed them in a tan colored bag. Finally, when I returned, I chopped lumber for the warmth of the hearth.

"Why have you done all these tasks when all I needed was wood?" the lady asked.

"Winter is upon us, and I wanted to help you prepare, that is all."

"I am grateful for your kindness." The old lady sat down and drank mint tea then she said, "Go back to the mill of John and in three days, I will send you the finest steed that your eyes shall ever see."

My eyes widened in surprise and I was at a loss for words. I picked up my bag and with a smile I began to walk out of the hut. I was overjoyed, trusting the old lady, I walked backwards waving my hand to her. By afternoon of the same day I reached the road that lead to the mill and by dusk I was sleeping in my bed.

The next morning, I resumed my chores at the mill. I began the daily routine when Jack and Jim arrived sooner than expected, each with a horse. I observed that each horse resembled the complexion of the one who acquired it.

Jack found a big and strong horse, when John looked at it, he commented, "This beast of a horse is great for heavy duty!" Jim, on the other hand, had a skinny horse to offer, "Well, well, this looks like a racing horse!" so said John, but then pondered for a moment then said, I have no idea! Both are great!"

When I approached them, John noticed I was back. "Oh, dear. Where is your horse Yrian?" He asked, more worried about the horse than what I had to say about the mill.

"It will be here in three days sir, by the way the mill requires mainte-nance, I need to acquire some pieces from town," I replied confidently.

The pair of buffoons began to laugh and make fun of me, "Three days, what is the meaning of this? Is your horse that slow that it got lost?"

John interrupted the jokes saying, "I see no problem; besides, three days is plenty to decide between these two horses and in the end I can better judge from the last two. Let us be fair in the contest. In the meantime," John paused and to my surprise handed Jack and Jim an apron saying, "let's get back to work, there is much to be done, and Yrian go fetch those items we need." Jack and Jim grunted, unhappy that they had to work.

The next three days were like any other day, except that John had not fully decided between the strong horse and the race horse. "The big horse will be able to hold me in case I start growing sideways. Wait, what am I saying? It is obvious I have to get slim now that I will retire, the racing horse will allow me to travel fast. Except, I will not be able to enjoy the good food. Hmm… which one which one?" John's reasoning for choosing a horse always concluded with, "Whatever, they are both great!" In addition, if the other two were not complaining about work, they were making jokes about me.

Upon the third morning there was music from trumpets and clarinets and a hasty sound of chariot wheels, announcing the entrance of an elegant blue chariot. It stopped outside the mill. John, Jack, and Jim were amazed. As for me, I did not notice because I was busy working.

The princes inside the chariot poked her beautiful visage out of the window and the three made a reverent gesture, greeting her. John asked, "Yes, your highness? What brings you here?"

"Where is your trusted servant?" the princes questioned.

"At your service!" replied Jack and Jim at the same time.

"Such beauty! That stallion is just like the one I have always dreamed of!" John rushed to stand next to the stable waiter holding the reins of a white horse and a pink dot on its nose. When John approached, he began to cares the stallion on its nose and the hair on top, he exhaled saying, "This is the most magnificent horse that my eyes have ever seen!"

"There he is! The one I have been looking for is the one holding a sack of flour!" she exclaimed, stepping out of the carriage to have a better view.

Two guards began to march in my direction to escort me to the princess. Once I stood in her presence, I asked with confusion, "How can I be of service?"

"I am the old lady of the forest," she paused and giggled, "well, I was. You see noble laborer, your kindness broke the spell of an evil warlock, now I have been restored to be a princess once more. Since I wish to repay you, I give you the horse I promised."

Turning the reigns of the stallion over to John I said, "This is the horse I have to offer."

"Indeed, this is the greatest horse in the whole world, no doubt. Hence, the mill and all that it is entitled now belongs to you Yrian!" John replied full of joy as his dreams were realized.

"Yrian wait," the princess interrupted, "leave the mill behind and come along with me. You were kind and served an old, wrinkly and ugly lady, you surely deserve to live happy!" The princess held out her hand and I held hers, stepping inside her carriage.

"John, thank you for everything, I wish you a great retirement, I will see what the princess has to further offer me." I said, ready to leave.

"Well then, we can't just stand here," said John as I stepped into the carriage, "I now have to judge who among the two is the hardest worker, and it is he who will earn the mill!" Jack and Jim were now in the best position, for one of them was going to inherit the mill. Kindness aside, this was the first time they both began to work.

My life was about to change. Out of nowhere, a princess arrived to change my daily routine. In all I did not know what to expect. The first few minutes on the road were silent, but she did smile and giggle. Then I dared to ask, "What is your name princess?"

"My apologies, I have just become aware that I never did properly introduce myself. I am princess Flora."

"How is it that you became an old lady?"

"The evil sorcerer Malgar, he used to be my father's advisor or so I am told, for I never met my parents. My father died and Malgar sought to gain power after. He was mistaken to think that one as beautiful such as me would marry him. Therefore, he transformed me into a hideous and wrinkly old lady!" she concluded with a greater tone. Clearly, she did not like the idea of being old. With a change in tone she continued, "But all of that has changed. I am free of his malevolence."

"What sort of spell did he cast upon you?"

"You mean to say: how the spell was lifted? He said that someone with kindness and the ability to see past my wretched vanity shall be able to set me free," she leaned closer towards me, "I was afraid because people like that are hard to come by."

The carriage halted and one of the attendants opened the door saying, "We have arrived at your palace, princess." Flora stepped down swiftly and I followed slowly. I was mesmerized, for my eyes had never seen a castle before. The courtyard was a big square; a path was decorated with grass and flowers leading to the main entrance. "Come along!" princess Flora turned and shouted with a gracious voice from the stairs that lead to the main hall while I was still in the courtyard.

The inside was even more colorful and fully decorated with banners with the coat of arms of Flora's family crest, resembling a clover and a Fleur-de-Lys. There were heads of animals I never thought existed, furniture, knight's armor, and weapons displayed across the hall.

Once in the throne room the princess rushed to embrace a young, dashing prince exclaiming, "My sweet Robert!" He lifted her, spinning her around, ending with a kiss.

"I do not know why you left, I missed you!" The man named Robert said to the princess once they kissed, staring at each other.

"Sweet Robert, I told you I had to pay a debt and I am a woman of my word."

"Who is this stranger you bring into the palace?" Robert said with disgust in his voice.

"This is the peasant who helped me," she responded, turning from Robert's eyes to look at me. "I brought him because he is a great worker."

She expected me to say something, but there was a moment of silence until she stated, "Because that is what you are good at: working diligently without being told to, right?"

I was shocked, not because of what the princess said, but because I did not know what I was supposed to do in the first place. My blank expression likewise made the princess and Robert confused.

"Well, the butler will be with you shortly to instruct you on your new chores," Flora finally said, walking away with Robert.

"You think that because a princess brings you to the palace that she will end up with someone like you?" said a new voice, as I turned, I saw the butler. My jaw was wide open, as I casually turned to face him, the butler's expression changed from sarcastic to confused for I was truly oblivious to the situation.

"I..." I stumbled on my words, "truly I have no idea what to do."

The butler addressed the princess who was already on the balcony of the next floor overlooking the throne room saying, "The peasant does not know what to do!"

Robert leaned forward to reply, "He is useless, get rid of him!"

"Perhaps I was mistaken." Flora added: "It seems appearances are deceiving." She then addressed the butler, "Please escort him out, he was not what I expected."

"My lady!" I exclaimed loudly as the princess began to turn away. I waited a moment, making sure I had her attention. "With my earnings of working in the mill I request the purchase of a farm. That way I can be of service to your kingdom."

Princess Flora was silent but Robert answered for her, "Give the man what he wants! He lifted your curse, this way he does not leave empty handed but remains a peasant such as he is."

She wanted to say something but stumbled, finally concluding: "I don't see why not, the butler will compensate for you, farewell."

When the two royals were out of view, I approached the butler saying, "Will you be so kind as to show me the land accessible for purchase?" Now the butler was the one looking confused. He brought some parchments and began to consult them, with a map signaling the available options. To my surprise, he did not mock me any further during the process. I opted for the section furthest away from town; distant enough to be away from the fast-paced society of a town but close enough to travel for supplies.

"How do you intend to pay?" The butler asked when we finalized the process.

"Make the bill payable to John the miller. I will write him a letter asking him to give you my earnings for the years I worked with him."

"With this document and this royal seal, you are now a land owner."

CHAPTER V

❧❧

Such it was that I became a farmer the moment I stepped outside the palace. The title and royal document allowed me to make any necessary purchases in order to start up my farm. Therefore, my next stop was the town center to acquire a cart and an ox. With those I could transport all necessary materials to develop the farm. On my way to the land, I stopped at the inn to eat.

Once I entered the inn, there was an argument involving a foreigner. "No! I don't care! If you do not have the means to pay you will not eat!" said the owner of the inn to a stranger.

"I do not seek the best meal, just what you can give. I can replay by cleaning and being in your service," replied the stranger with a foreign accent, one I had not heard before.

"Leave! I have no use of beggars; besides, I already have someone who cleans."

"I understand, I bid you a pleasant day," said the stranger, bowing down. When he turned around, I noticed he looked different, not European but as if he was from a distant continent. I was standing in the door and the stranger asked me to move saying, "Please excuse me."

Stepping aside, I inquired, "How long has it been since you last had a meal?"

"Not long, just a few days, but it is hard when one wanders, looking for a place to work."

"I was looking for a place to eat, but it seems the inn has reached its maximum capacity. Would you like to ride with me and allow me to buy you a meal?"

"I will be honored to share a meal with a kind person such as you."

Once on the cart, I introduced myself, "My name is Yrian, by the way."

"A pleasure, I am Junichi, humble poet of the far east in Japan."

Along the way to town I began to inquire about Japan, where Junichi answered beyond my questions. I was surprised because at first glance he looked quiet and reserved. Through our meal, the Japanese man did not seem to hide any information, then again, I restrained myself from asking personal questions. He finally concluded saying, "How can I repay you for this meal?"

"There is nothing to repay, I simply noticed you were hungry and weary. Besides, your company was pleasant and I learned something new today."

"I must be of service in some way." Junichi insisted, again referring to service.

"Junichi, allow me to ask: what is the meaning of service where you come from?"

To my surprise, Junichi looked down, leaning back on the chair, raising his lip, his expression pondering how to answer or not, replying with silence. "I apologize if I asked a personal question, you do not have to answer." I said.

"It's fine, it is just that I have not meditated on this matter for a long time. It has become clear that I can not escape whom I really am." Junichi said still looking at the floor, and then found my eyes again to answer. "I was a samurai, a soldier whose sole duty is to serve."

"Now you are trying to escape your past?"

"That life is no longer, yet I can not deny the part of me that longs to serve. When a samurai loses their master, they become ronin or a wanderer. I am no longer a warrior I am a poet, but I am a wanderer that seeks to serve others."

"It must be hard to abandon a life of service like that of a soldier and remain motivated to find a purpose that is much simpler." Junichi nodded at my remark with silence.

Trying to help, I said, "Junichi, if it helps, I am on my way to build a farm. Just today I received the documents entitled to the ownership. That is why I have the cart full of materials and honestly, I will need some help to finish before the winter. I may not be able to pay you, but I can offer you food and my company."

"Say no more Yrian, I will be honored to serve you and help you from now until you no longer need me."

"Thank you, Junichi, but please do not see me nor treat me like your master, see me as your friend." He bowed down and I returned the gesture. Lo and behold, began my friendship with Junichi.

The months preceding winter served for further exploration regarding the samurai's past. With concealed sadness he opened his heart, and told me about Riko; as a samurai he was devoted to her, as a man his heart wanted to be at her service. "I have no regrets; three years have passed and I embrace her passing with honor."

"Do you still think of her, of what could have been?"

"I can not love someone who is dead, but to answer your question, I no longer believe in love."

"Junichi, the Shogun certainly lied so you will not take revenge upon him, if you survived, I believe she might have as well."

"That is the past Yrian, Riko is not my present, I have to set a path for my future." Such was Junichi's point of view and we did not talk any further about Riko or the life of a samurai.

CHAPTER VI

❧ ❧

This season of winter was the longest in many years, as harsh as it was, I contracted an incurable flu. My body ached; my temperature rose to boil my head and the sneezing kept me from sleeping. When I was able to sleep, my lungs desperately needed air that my nose was not able to provide. In trying to fight the disease with minimal activity, I realized my breath was short. During this time, Junichi did not leave my side, always caring in my time of need.

"I am at your service and friendship is the greatest form of benevolent duty," Junichi told me one night when I asked why he attended to me. I was sincerely grateful.

The seemingly unending freeze finally came to pass and my health was almost restored. I worked without fainting or gasping to catch a breath, but it was a burden to sleep.

Junichi returned one day from town to inform me that he had set an appointment with a renowned and highly recommended doctor. "The medic travels from towns, castles, and villages to cure the impossible." This doctor was clearly in the limelight, when we arrived to her consulting room it was crowded with a multitude of ill people. Half the town was at her doorstep because within the end of the month, she was going to be in her next location. The wait was long, but every person walking out was healthier than when they first entered.

"Up next is Yrian." I heard my name called and walked in to see a young maiden with golden brown, long curly hair.

"What ill brings you here?" The moment she turned around and I gazed into her eyes all malady that I felt vanished. Instantly I was fully revitalized. "Did the mouse steal your cheese or did a cat bite your tongue?" In a sweet, gentle voice she smiled and continued.

"I caught a cold at the start of the winter season," I answered, ending with a cough and covering my mouth.

"Cof, cof," she replied in a playful tone, handing me some water. "That is usual, remember to drink all the water you can and for your infection take these," she gave me a leaf with thorns. "Let the plant grow, when its edges are long, cut them and drink the liquid that pours out, make tea out of the rest of the leaf," she then approached me to walk me out.

"Can I ask your name doctor?" I asked before leaving.

"My name is Portia," the gentle doctor answered with a smile.

I took a deep breath, as I exhaled, I repeated her name, "Portia, it was nice to meet you."

She blushed a little and said, "I hope you feel better," then called her next patient.

The next morning I rushed to the consulting room to greet doctor Portia. I arrived before she began work, she was attending some plants in a garden. "You are up early! Should you not be resting?" She set aside the green water can she was using, "Your name is Yrian, correct?"

I cleared my throat and began to recite my 'Unusual Remedy:'

> I sought medical care to my achy fever,
> The cough did not stop. End this mad disease!
> Reason meld with pain is but a breather,
> Constant, and to no avail unfreezes.
> More than a physician to my love art thou

For reason's prescription caused sorrow and pain.
Thy presence is more than I can allow,
It lifts me high in the air like a crane.
Glimmering light that shines upon me, hope
Is my present care that causes no unrest.
Examine me using a microscope,
See the truth I have approached to confess.
Am I sick with an incurable flue?
I came for a cure, but now, I see you."

Portia stood straighter, revealing her tall figure, walked closer to me and said, "Is that so, that a fair maiden is your cure? Had I not been flattered by your sweet words I dare say it was love that cured you?"

"In all sincerity my lady, I wish to know more about you, gentle Portia and who she is."

"One day I will like to have a family of my own, but be advised, he who choseth me, must give and hazard all he hath, for my profession keeps me busy."

"Is love not threatening, and the outcome as dangerous as all the fair promises with no compromise? In such case, I dare respond that by choosing not from the view of outer appearance such as it is beauty, may not result in what many men desire nor as much as they deserve, but the reward is fortune and bliss."

"Well spoken, young sir, but how do I know that your words are as true as the disposition within your heart?"

"I am a humble farmer. I am not from noble birth and certainly not brave like a gallant knight. I am learned and have read scrolls of old and books alike— such as the testament of heroes as they were told; yet I do not see myself upon the list. However, I realize why those heroes are acclaimed, because their deeds are defined by their inner purpose, such is why they venture through hardship and pain. Those stories have meaning to me and guide me to build the character of who I want to be." I paused because Portia turned her glance from me as a red cardinal landed on her left shoulder. She held it gently and said, "This red belly bird is my messenger. It tells me that the patients will arrive soon."

"Then I shall take my leave."

Portia lifted the cardinal and it took flight. She then stepped closer to me. In a whisper she said, "In simple words how will you summarize your purpose?"

Without hesitation I said, "You are my quest."

Looking me in the eyes she replied, "Return before sunset, and I will tell you all you wish about Portia."

Before the hour of twilight, I returned to the appointment room with a flower. When Portia was done for the day she walked out and smiled saying, "So far you are on the right track."

"How was your day?"

"It was long and a hassle, but I enjoy the process. So, tell me what do you have in mind?"

"I think that if we reach that hill in time, I will show you a beautiful sunset." We climbed the hill that overlooked the town to marvel at the colors in the sky. First orange, followed by blue, and finally purple. Just before dusk turned to dark, I spotted two eagles. I signaled Portia to follow my sight with my finger, "Look to the right my lady! Two hunters of the sky sharing flight."

"I have never seen two eagles so close before. Oh look! They have joined in free fall!"

"Out of all the courtship rituals in the animal kingdom this is the greatest, for the eagles soar to a dizzying altitude only to embrace and fall, separating at the last moment."

Portia turned her eyes from the spectacle in the sky to find mine. I finished watching the eagles and turned to find her eyes. Locked in her eyes, I simply stood still trying not to blink.

"Why do you look at me like that?" she questioned.

"I do not know if you are beautiful because I have not gotten past your eyes."

"One day you might find out," she concluded.

"That is an unknown just like how mysterious life can be, but I do not need all the answers so long as my eyes find yours."

Portia smiled and looked at the horizon again. She exhaled saying, "I relish at the colors of the sunset and this has been the most magical so far. I am glad you brought me here."

We began our descent from the hill and walked back to her establishment. The following days we explored the town, going to the gardens, walking along the river until one night she invited me into her house for dinner where I learned more about her.

"Tell me Yrian, for the last month you have not asked me how I wish to be loved, you have not attempted to grab my hand nor kiss me." Portia stated, serving me a dish of salmon.

"I do not think it is proper, I believe that there is a process for things to develop. One can not rush the growth of corn just because one is hungry."

"Often times in life we wish for things to happen instantly, without first taking into consideration the process. So says a doctor, who wishes all diseases were cured instantly."

"Tell me sweet Portia, why did you become a doctor?"

She finished setting the table, sat down, and gave thanks for the meal, company, and blessings to her family, then answered me, "Doctors are the profession of my family. My simple answer is that I want to follow in my father's footsteps."

"What will be the elaborate side of choosing to be a doctor and not a lady who plans masquerade dances, and sits at home waiting for her knight in shining armor to return from the crusade?"

"You mean to say I am not a noble lady?" She pulled out a green fan and used it to cover her face.

I could not help but laugh, when I finally regained my composure I said, "It is not common to find a lady as independent such at yourself, who works for her wellbeing in service towards others." I paused, letting my smile remain.

"Rarely do we attend to our health, only when it is too late. I did not get the chance to meet my grandfather; he died when my father was young due to smoking, my father offered to help my grandmother and his brothers while studying and practicing to become a doctor. When I was twelve and learned my family's history, my purpose became clear, to treat medicine not only on the physical level but the soul as well as Plato would say. Now Yrian, tell me why you became a farmer."

"I was about five when my parents sent me from Scandinavia to work in a mill. I recently became a farmer because I like to see plants grow, the care I give to my work grants me results and provides for me."

We concluded dinner and talked until midnight when I thanked Portia for the meal and bid her a good night. Before walking out, she embraced me and thanked me for the moments we shared during the month. I tried to lean closer to kiss her but she said, "Let our feelings grow until they bear fruit, then I will correspond with what you seek from me."

"I am glad I was able to plant a seed in your heart, dear Portia. If there is a way to tend to any emotional needs, know that I am always here." I left her embrace and began to walk in the direction of my farm.

The next morning, I arrived before dawn to wish Portia a good day but instead found a scroll on the door handle reading:

Dear Yrian,
This last month was memorable. I am glad that you gave me a change of pace in my routine. Thank you for your company. I will wait eagerly to see you next year, even if it sounds distant.
Yours truly, Portia.

A tear streamed out of my right eye, when I finished reading, I kissed the letter and pressed it hard upon my heart. I looked up at the treed surrounding the empty house that by this time was filled with people, then into the sky. When my glance returned down, I spotted the red belly cardinal on top of the house. Holding my tears, I said to the bird: "Please tell Portia how much she means to me."

CHAPTER VII

᠄ᡪᡐ

D ays turned to weeks and weeks into months and finally a
year, but there was no news from Portia. Junichi noticed my
lack of morale but after two months he told me: "Venture into
the forest. Let your mind free and revitalize your spirit. Do not
worry about the farm, I will look after it."

I did not try to disagree and set out for adventure. I planned
to be gone less than a week, but there were other events in
store for me. This is when I met Harold and Gerald, whom
were eager to demonstrate their skills and aspired to be heroes. It was that morning our paths crossed. The two brothers
were out on adventures whereas I simply wanted to enjoy a
nature walk.

"Come with us!" ordered Harold the moment I saw them.
Both had a scary, commanding presence and thus I decided not
to contradict them. Short after, we came across a massive anthill.

"This pile of dirt is on our way brother," said Harold, "ob-
serve as I clear the path with my spear!"

The ants began to move in disarray, but before any harm was
done, I rushed to stand in front of Harold saying desperately:
"Please don't, I love ants!"

With a coy smile the pompous, young prince stopped. The three of us carried on when next we came across a lake and a duck sitting on a rock. This time Gerald said, "I am hungry and I was not aware that it was duck season! I will shoot this creature with my crossbow and eat it for lunch!

Gerald was taking aim when I once again intervened, "Please hold, the family of this duck is nearby! I will prepare lunch instead." Thankfully, the prince stopped. I opened my sack and prepared a vegetable stew for the hungry prince. It did not take long for the brothers to intended to harm nature when Gerald, annoyed by the buzzing of a bee flying around nearby flowers stood up and stamped his foot all over the flowers.

"Hold on! Bees are friendly!"

"Why do you always halt us?" Harold demanded.

I turned around to face Harold and told him, "Bees pollinate most of the crop species essential to a farmer and the plants that other animals eat. We need them as much as they need our care."

"Do not be mad brother, the peasant has a point." Gerald walked around my side and stood next to Harold and continued, "Otherwise, how would you drink mead without honey?" The mockery ended with a hysterical laugh.

The next stop on my forced journey with the two brothers was an old castle, abandoned in the middle of the forest. "Let us see who dwells inside and meet the lord," Harold said. He was about to knock when Gerald pushed the door open stating, "This place is desolate, leave the knocking to the peasant, we are royalty and do as we please."

"Anyone mind welcoming two noblemen into this castle?" shouted Harold across the dark halls filled with spider webs that did not reply as we entered.

The main hall was an amazing scene: nobles were dining in a long, extended table and musicians played while the rest of the court danced, yet all were motionless, their moment captured in stone. One was drinking, another standing as if proclaiming a toast, but all in stone. Each stone looked as if it were carved out of marble, facial features from moles to wrinkles, but they were petrified.

"This place is enchanted!" Harold exclaimed, and for the first time I heard a difference in his tone of voice.

"I am going home!" I said turning around as a shiver ran down my spine, the feeling in likeness to a worm crawling down my back.

"Stay here!" Gerald prevented me from leaving, dragging me from the back of my vest.

"You are correct to leave in time," exclaimed a mysterious voice and the three of us began to look where the voice came from. "Down here," said the same voice, as we followed the first echo away from the main hall into the stairs leading down the main entrance.

"Behold, a real dwarf!" Gerald screamed pointing with his finger while extending his posture back, his face in shock at the sight.

"Correction, I am a gnome and I have been in this castle long enough to know its secrets. There is a spell whirling about: who so ever brakes the spell will be a hero—the savior of the people trapped in stone."

The three of us were confused but Harold stepped up saying, "I shall be the one to undo the spell."

"Very well," said the gnome with his old, rusty voice. "Go to the forest and find a thousand pearls that are missing, when you do bring them back to me."

So Harold set out into the center of the forest. He looked for the pearls all afternoon, but failed to find a single one. Exhausted and soaked in sweat he returned empty handed saying, "The task is impossible."

"Grrr, nothing," The gnome began to shake from side to side, his expression angry until he paused and in a normal tone concluded, "is impossible!" The instant the little gnome turned away, Harold froze, becoming a stone. He then walked towards Gerald telling him with a voice that resonated with great importance, "You shall indeed succeed were your brother has failed. Go forth to the lake, retrieve the golden key that is in its depths and bring it back."

Without question Gerald set out to the lake and plunged himself in its waters, diving to the depths. He searched with every breath until his lungs surrendered. In a failed attempt, likewise returned empty handed before the sky turned dark. "Impossible to find a key on a grand lake!" Said Gerald, soaking wet, trying to find air for his lungs.

"Nothing is impossible!" protested the gnome and Gerald turned to stone.

At the sight of these events unfolding in less than a day I did not wish to join the brothers, so I chose to sneak away from the castle. Instantly I heard a loud tapping. The gnome stood on a ledge above me with his arms crossed, his small foot making the loud noise.

"Your time has come. It is now your turn." The gnome said impatiently with his projected voice.

"I'd rather let this opportunity pass." Trying to hide my nerves I replied, "I gladly pass down this task to one more deserving to be named a hero!"

"I do not want to hear excuses!" The gnome lowered both hands in response and lifted himself with a jump demanding, "You will try!"

The gnome began to push me to the door where the two princes before me had left in excitement, only to return in shame. Looking at the door and my fate foreshadowed in stone I shouted, "I demand a trial by poetry!"

"What?" the gnome halted confused, "Reciting poesy will not undo the spell!"

In my defense I said,

"Bitter sweetness is my taste
In longing for the one who is far
In a distant land. I must haste
To pour out my heart inside a jar.
I fear to utter my thoughts, for this scar
Of past afflictions I wish not to explore.
I prefer sorrow, than make you my star.
Yet a voice urges me to roar.

So before I fall again I shall soar
To stand next to thee my dear.
My verses shall lay till the days of yore.
Surrender to my virtue, let us rejoice without fear.
May is near, behold the hero comes home,
To stay in a place that gives him hope."

The gnome responded,

"Repeat, repeat, and repeat
Is the sound that echoes
And repeats.
Of recycled word
Spoken over again.

Speak, speak, and speak
What have thou said?
Please repeat what was told
Of quotes lost of their sound.

Repetition, repetition, repetition
What is the meaning of repeating?
What is thy dialogued petition?

Once again, once again, once again
The repetitive resound is heard once more;
Like a duplicate recall that resonates in vibrant ears.

Communicate, communicate, communicate
For no words may be heard.
A speechless mouth be that who speaks.
Utter a verbalized, yet an articulated lecture,
Which must be properly addressed,
In a manner of satisfied speaking

Of oral communication
Of oral language;
Not yet withstanding
Of lacking whispers and mumbling voiceless.

Words absent of worth and diction.
If thus be not so...
Then a repetition
Without petition
Will be made."

Then my turn came,

"T"is more than a sight of thine heavenly eyes.
By the action of absence I miss thy company.
Distance grants me virtue. Patience is my reprise
So that I may support thee wondrously.
And day after day, by my honor I testify:
Thou ar't the quest by which now I am realized."

The gnome now smiled and asked,
"Do not let her go.
Do not let her go, I tell you.
Who is she
Who holds thy heart
And leaves without saying goodbye?"

To which I replied,
"May I compare thee next to a flower's
Inner beauty? As a rose I saw,
Resting in the river's rapid flow.
Sprouting in hardship, t'was my thought.
Hummingbirds and bees admire thy roots.
Moving with the creek, like a serenade

Time holds still, for thou art beauty in minutes
For the stream strikes hard, and thou does not decay.
Abundance of water is no place for
A plant to grow. Beyond vegetation,
And the reach of my embrace. Calm nor
Patient is thy love. My affection
Shall have to wait, for I admire thy beauty
From afar; my virtue for thee, is my fidelity."

Changing his tone, the gnome responded:

"Sorrow not go with pain
As I contemplate Martial's epigram,
Seeking the ideal life, I wish to attain.
My inner self is holding kilograms
Worth of verses that seek to sing.
I read Sidney and it makes me think
Of a Libyan dream I found in spring.
As I blink, she fades and I shrink.
Alas this angel is a muse that aids
In the writing of my thoughts in verse,
Come to memory, you are but a shade,
Seeing you again will only make me worse.
But reading Spenser fills my visage with hope
That I will grow old in a greater scope."

I carried on,

"A keen sense of ethical conduct surrounds thy grace,
Abide by the respect he deserves
For his complexion, is that of a royal embrace.
The integrity of the man, knight or samurai is not great,
But rather it is an exalted aggrandize.
His manners are worth more than a golden plate.

Enunciated words clash before thy ears
With the sharpness of a Katana sword.
His finer veracity is more than it appears.
The glorification can only be that of truth.
Naught is regarded with more respect,
For only truth is fountain of youth.
By my troth I pray this values be true.
Be they not, it was just a déjà vu."

The gnome impatiently recited,

"The present moon yields to the sun.
My hopes and dreams are stolen by your devotion.
I have fallen from grace to pursue you in vain, Oh! I am done.
Behold my divine angel who shows no emotion.
The sands of time are ticking by in stone.
My profanity composes words, to think of you is a vice.
You overcame my thought and your desire.
Your absence and silence, are my dreams on fire
Scorching my hopes of seeing your hidden smile.
I implore to comply my feelings with no force.
I now exhort forgiveness and bid you a safe course."

The little man concluded, signaling me to the exit.
No sooner I recited only for the gnome to interrupt, but a limerick arose,

"Once in a faraway land
There once was a knight that was grand."

"A maid did he spy.
And said 'hi.'
And she ran away through the sand."

"Once in a faraway land
There once was a knight that was grand."

"Whose gaze fell upon
The daughter of John
And along came a new wedding band."

The gnome walked closer to me and I stated my intentions in verse,

"Oh pondering heart, pondering mind,
Embrace me like a star, to stand by her side.

I have to lose my pride. My heart's desire is out of reach.
Like fruits, I have lost the taste of peach."

The gnome looked up to me and said,

"Hope is always present...
Hope never deserts a Nobel cause.
For when all goes to void; never despair
There is always hope!
Now fetch me the stones."

"So..." I stood still, "What task shall I undertake?"
"Find the pearls." Answered he directly and simply.
"The pearls?" I repeated, afraid. The gnome began to tap his foot and closing his eyes, nodded.

I raised my eyebrows, pressed my lips together, inhaled and exhaled taking my first step, which turned to many steps as I reluctantly began the search. My luck was no different. All I found were rocks, trees, and piles of dirt. Finally, I sat down to look at the sunset from a hill overlooking the castle, the lake and hills where the sun was setting. I imagined being next to Portia and sadness took me, first my throat dried up, my eyes watered, I lowered my head to my knees and I began to cry. I feared I was never going to see her again.

Then ants began to march in my direction and moved about to create words. It read: "You saved our hill and now we shall help you." Moments later they appeared in great numbers with the pears! I put them in a bag, thanked the ants for arriving in my time of need and hurried back to the castle.

"Here little one! I have the missing pearls!"

"Wonderful!" exclaimed the gnome. "Now bring me the golden key from the lake."

"But, I do not know how to swim!"

"No 'buts,'" said the gnome pushing me out of the castle forcefully and slamming the door.

I lit up a torch and went to the lake. I circled the lake, contemplating, and stared at the glimmer of the moon reflected on its surface. When I was about to admit defeat a duck appeared, with its beak holding a stick it began to write on the dirt: "You saved me and my family. In return, I will save you."

"How can you save me?"

"Quack, quack," said the duck and dived into the water. Shortly it emerged with the golden key, glittering with the moonlight.

"Thank you, dear duck!" Jovial, I ran to the castle thinking the challenge to be over. "Here is the key! Can I go home now?"

"No, no, no, there is one final task reserved just for you, but we shall wait until morning, rest for now." The gnome led me to a chamber, lit a candle, and bid me a good rest. The thought of what awaited me did not prevent me from sleeping soundly, for the next morning the gnome entered the room, pulled the covers of the bead saying loudly, "Wake up, wake up! It's time for your final task!" He then led me to a beautiful garden in the back of the castle."You must find the flower with the sweetest nectar." Said the gnome closing his eyes, inhaling the overwhelming scent of flowers.

"Really? What about the pearls, and the key?" I asked reluctantly. "You have to save those who came before you and your own fate. So, commence your search."

Smelling daisy, lily, carnation, tulips to rose, my nose soon was unable to distinguish among the variety of flowers in the garden.

"Who can possibly find the flower that stands out from all the rest?"

There was a buzzing noise and when I looked up there was a queen bee, "I flew all this way just to give you thanks for saving my hive. Likewise, I shall assist you in your search." said she and began to fly from flower to flower, tasting their nectar, until finally exclaiming, "Delicious! This nectar is delectable!" I thanked the bee for guiding me to select the correct flower, and presented it to the gnome.

"Oh my! Somehow I knew you had to triumph!" he replied, jumping and clapping. The moment he sniffed the flower, a cloud of dust covered the gnome and with a puff of smoke he was transformed to a tall king.

The monarch turned to find my eyes and said, "You have broken the spell!" All who were captured in stone came back to life that present moment. The two young princes whom I began the journey approached me, Harold was first to speak, "We believed that we had the qualities to become heroes, but we were mistaken. Being the eldest son, I had pride as my ally. Now I seek humility, for this, I shall repent and go to the Middle East and join the crusades."

"Thank you noble Yrian for your actions. I will retire, this kind of life does not suit me," said Gerald. The monarch gave each one a sack of gold in compensation as each brother left the castle on a different road.

The king invited me to join him in the main hall to feast. I questioned the monarch to learn more about him and the spell, "Tell me great king, how is it that your castle fell under such a spell?"

"Once upon a time, this was a beautiful kingdom, then came a witch and forever cursed me. She said I would live to witness the rise and fall of my own emotional life. It began with an empty feeling like the void overshadowing my heart and thoughts. I can still feel the ache. No sun can brighten this feeling for I am haunted by my past memories and events. Then a warlock appeared, asking for a moment in time, he cursed my kingdom, turning all to stone."

"Can you explain how you turned into a gnome?"

"I do not know if I have the heart to tell you, for it haunts me to this day despite all malice that has been lifted." The king paused before resuming his tale. "I am going in circles, I have not been myself for some time. When everything was normal, before any curses and sorcery, I was a bachelor seeking love and a happy union for my kingdom. A red velvet rose, the shiny moon, a shooting star, an angel, and a maid in black represent that which I lost. For to pronounce their names shall bring ruin upon my heart."

So began the tale, 'The lost loves of the Bachelor"

The bachelor found flowers in a garden. A fragrance drew him towards a red Rose. Drawn by its texture, he was amazed. Yet in hugging the Rose, the thorns hidden within pierced his heart and his love was now lost. For he loved the Rose, she did not love him back, none was said but actions spoke as the thorns pierced his heart, and heartbroken he now lies.

Until our bachelor found the Moon, his nights brightened by a white spark. Like a rising tide he was drawn to this mystic source. Many nights he devoted to the Moon; but the Moon changes phases, and when the New Moon came by, his love became adieu, fare thee well, and goodbye. He tried to win her back but lacked, for the Moon's new face was no longer impressed.

A lone wolf, a florist with no flowers he became. Our bachelor never forgets those two who made an impact on his heart, wondering what they now think of him. Moving on, he still recalls those pretty maids who fail to leave his heart.

It may be true that a broken heart can only be repaired with love. Perhaps our bachelor must not open up on a first date for his heart has been broken many times before. He may only let in someone who really loves him so. He only prays that a miracle saves what he lost. Only to hope for the inevitable—to no avail he loses once more.

Among the lost lies the Fallen Star, as fair as million galaxies shining the void of space through light-years of confusion, she was in the back of his mind. Lacking any courage to let his love known, he truly lost his match. For she had found a galaxy of her own. Yet her love is a supernova, creating a new star and decimating what is on her path. To this day she will be lost in space.

In the past, he knew, the peace was calm and sweet. Letting his motives fly to be known to the world, a feeling strikes and harms where it hurts the most. What would be next? Only time may tell.

Burying his heart, he thought not to fall for Cupid's games. An Angel fell from heaven as a prisoner of her own heart. Using his charms, the bachelor unraveled the sweet side of the Angel. Knowing how forbidden his love for her could be, for the very first time he uttered the greatest sin of all, professing his love. The Angel could not bear this radical love upon herself.

The bachelor changed, letting go of selfish thoughts to see her point of view. Surrendering to her wishes, he kneeled to pray for her only to see her go in silence, such as the answer to all prayers. There is a secret between them; love tries to speak, yet morality drives them not to.

The bachelor withdrew to the desert. The heat removed all sense of serenity, his mind grew restless and no comfort appeased him.

On his journey out of the desert he found a mystical lamp. In a desperate attempt the bachelor gave the Genie all he posed, to find a way to reach the Angel left behind.

What the lost man did comprehend is that unrequited love could not be bought nor sought out by supernatural means. The bachelor lost all because he could not live with the agony of witnessing yet another beauteous maid leave his side. He can only see her in his dreams, and the image that he once had of her is slowly fading away, like a castle made of sand, will soon be washed away only to become part of the beach.

Until one day on the beach upon the hours of sundown a maiden began to walk towards him. At first nothing captivated him, but her company little by little began to soothe that broken spirit of his. Before the sun began to shine the next day, the maiden dismissed herself without first promising the bachelor to return in the evening. She departed by walking down to the ocean floor. While he awaited her return, for the first time in many years the bachelor felt his feelings had matured but was eager to explore.

It was when dusk approached and as the sun was setting, he saw how the maiden emerged from the salty waters. The water dripping down her skin, as she surfaced, she left behind a trace of scales. The bachelor soon learned that she was a mermaid and that each night she could walk on shore. That night they decided to swim. The bachelor and the mermaid both entranced one other.

Before sunrise he attempted to follow her at the cost of drowning, hoping to receive a kiss from the mermaid. For it is said by sailors, that only a mermaid's kiss, can keep one from drowning. The bachelor swam with all his strength, but the lack of air made him drowsy and so he passed out. When next he opened

es, he was back on the beach. The mermaid had brought
back. She told him that she tried to make him a part of her
world, but sadly he could not be. The bachelor came close to
realizing his aspirations. Alas, he would not comply with the
mermaid for he had previously poured out all his emotions and
thus his heart was dry. The swim had fatigued him and with no
oxygen he could not think. He only listened and when all was
said, he simply saw her in sadness and tears, trying to swim
back to the ocean like a floppy fish refusing help.

A day arrived when he married and life turned to bliss, only for
his wife to die in childbirth, left alone to wander the world and
take care of a motherless daughter. A woman appeared dressed
in black, punctual to the emotional wake of the bachelor. She
came out the murky corner of his heart, soothing the pain, while
adding a layer of mystery. Her presence was but a puzzling sensation, that if it were simple to explain, it will remain undeveloped.
Truth be told, in forgetting about his Angel, whom had terrified
the feelings of the Bachelor, in order to understand the ebony
maiden, the bachelor replaced her image with that of the Angel
becoming thus, but a shadow of his innermost desire.

They were opposites, he was day and she was night. He was
glad and she was sad, he dressed with an array of colors and she
dressed to mourn. He brought the light where she resisted him.
In the end she departed, turning the bachelor into a gnome in a
funeral for his dead emotions.

"Now tell me, how was it that you accomplished the impossible
on three occasions?" said the king when he concluded.

"When there are friends in gratitude, nothing is impossible. Even
your hardships now my lord, you can enjoy happiness that your
kingdom has been restored."

"In peace and prosperity yes, in matters of the heart, nay. I do not believe in love anymore. I will live to see the last days of my house with no heir on this forsaken land. Nor see my daughter grow, she is gone, and what little hope I had of ever seeing her again is left in the past, I doubt she will recognize me if she saw me." The king concluded, and I did not question him further. The solitude he felt was no different than before the spell vanished. There was music, food, and the court jester made others laugh but the king remained silent for the remainder of dinner.

CHAPTER VIII

❧ ⚜ ❧

The next morning I departed back to my farm. The melancholy sight of the monarch haunted me in the coming year. I stopped seeing the red belly bird, my activities did not bring me joy, and moreover I began to question my ideals, but one question in particular: Did I have the strength and patience to wait for Portia?

It was a sunny morning, the rooster crowed, the cow and horses created an ambient sound, a farmer's delight to start their day. I was planting vegetables when I was interrupted by a courier, "I have been looking all over for you!" He reached into his satchel, "I have something I have to deliver—your hands only. Let's see here: It's from a friend, well that was it, now I have to go." Just as he came to give me the letter, he left.

The letter was from Portia! My heart began to beat faster, all my attention fixed on the letter. My fist question was—why did she not send the red bird? I was shocked; it was not even a letter more of a note reading: "During our interactions, although brief, I realized that all I can offer you is a friendship. I am sure there is someone special for you. Farewell."

I placed the note back in the envelope and dropped it in the mud and began to walk forward, my eyes not focused on the sky, the ground, the trees, simply on the note. What would a hero do in my position? Rush to his maiden and profess his love, perhaps offer her gifts or say: "I am here for you?" Despite the urge to seek her out, the truth remained, that I was no hero and she was working, the profession of a physician is more demanding than that of a farmer.

"Do not feel bad Yrian," said Junichi as I turned around and saw him holding the muddied note. "Life continues despite our heartless mind longing for moments of the past."

"This note came to me as a surprise, nothing more."

"Yrian, I have been at your side three years, we have talked about farm life but rarely on matters of the heart and I blame myself for being closed to this subject." He moved closer to me and then continued, "The road of life is ahead, Portia is constantly moving from one town to the next, even though you are stationary as a farmer, waiting for crops to grow, do not wait for love."

"Why have you closed your heart, Junichi? When I first met you, I noticed that you were leaving your past behind. You have not spoken about your life in Japan ever since." I asked.

He was silent, and I simply looked at him. He finally said, "I lost the one person that gave my life meaning. Instead of dwelling in the past or what could have been, I decided to move forward."

"Follow your path without looking back, is that what life is all about? To me this is no different than traveling at night, with no light from fire or the full moon."

Junichi smiled responding, "I thought only the Japanese spoke in metaphor until I met you, please explain."

"The future is unknown and we venture towards it, leaving our past behind, not looking back." I began to walk backwards while still looking at Junichi saying, "What if instead we walked looking at the past, not necessary holding on, but rather as lessons for the future."

"Yrian," he took a deep breath and exhaled saying, "I am quiet and reserved on my past not because I want to escape it, nor because it pains me to think about it but rather because I simply left it where it belongs, the past. Let me ask you Yrian: are you making Portia the hope for your future?"

"As only a man looks at a woman, yes. It is my daydream to wait for the moment when I will next look upon her."

Junichi approached so to stand closer to me, "This note does not mean the end despite how you may feel. So long as both of you are alive, there is hope." Junichi cleaned off the mud and handed it to me, pressing it gently to my chest. "I say this because I do not see love the way you do Yrian, because the person I loved is dead." And he walked away to carry on.

We were silent for the rest of the day, working on the farm until that night we had unlikely visitors. Gerald and his brother Harold, who was in company of a lady, sought me out, as someone to trust and give them advice. The five of us sat around the campfire, the lady was the first to speak.

"Sometimes a kiss is a mystical interaction between two people. A magic that stops time, embraces you with joy, and makes you think of nothing but that person. I am Princess Emirah of the Arabian Desert, and this is the story of how I met prince Harold.

CHAPTER IX

❧ ❦

It began the summer I was to be married. My father, the sultan, summoned all legible suitors to my presence, unlike our traditions of arranged marriage, my father allowed me to select my husband.

Before bringing the suitors to the throne room my father introduced me to a knight. "Daughter, meet Harold, our ambassador from Europe. He will oversee relationships between our countries," my father said.

"I am told that there have been numerous outbreaks by rebels attempting to overthrow the caliphate, I am at your service, wise and noble ruler, in matters of security and diplomacy," said the gallant knight.

"I thank you prince, but my priority is for you to watch over my daughter. I am afraid my court has been infiltrated. My daughter's marriage is a political issue, with other caliphates trying to gain access to my nation, powerful families trying to enlarge their position, and rebels who are threatening what little order my family has established in the region. Those hallow suitors simply see my daughter as a possession, and my own walls are corrupted. As an outsider, untainted by my situation, with your fresh eyes and mind watch over her."

I'd never heard my father speak his mind so simply. In simplicity, confusion is found. In the past I argued with him about not wanting an arrange marriage, that I wanted love to be the prime reason for marriage, only for him to say: "Foolish girl, true love does not exist! Wake up to reality!" Now in the presence of a foreigner he simplified the situation: my value for marriage was merely political, and my father was overwhelmed by the politics.

"The suitors will soon arrive father, let us go to the throne room." I gently placed my right hand on his shoulder.

He turned and said, "Choosing one of them has consequences, and not choosing likewise has consequences. I only beg you make the right choice."

The three of us went to the throne room, where I sat next to my father and prince Harold stood at my side. A messenger arrived to introduce the ten suitors, three from local families, two unknown with a suspicious backgrounds, and five from other regions, ranging from Arabia, Persia, and even India.

"Welcome gentlemen to the kingdom of Aljusen, my father and I welcome you all," I stood and greeted them before my father or the messenger was able to introduce each and every one of them with their backstory, which I did not care to hear. "I am aware some of you come from distant regions but do know that I will know each and every one of you personally, conversing with each one, and in the end, I will announce the suitor I choose. I will begin with the one that has traveled the furthest."

The suitors looked at one another confused, one in disbelief, then one of them stepped closer saying, "I am Sai, from Bengal, India."

"Well Sai, step closer, the rest of you return tomorrow."

I began to question Sai, yet he began to interact with my father, changing my conversation. When I saw the suitor was tired, I moved us to dinner, I carried the conversation on to the history of him and his family.

"I am feeling nauseous," said the suitor moments later at dinner. "Retire to rest, your journey was a long one." I replied, and Sai simply fell asleep, without control over his own body, his head fell on the table. Harold was quick to grab the suitor so his face would not be damaged by the impact. I simply stood up and dismissed myself from the dining room.

This continued each day, meeting a new suitor only for them to fall asleep during dinner. On the fifth day Harold approached me saying, "Princess, I have noticed that for the past five days after dinner you sneak out of the palace."

"It must be someone else for I remain in my chambers."

"The behavior of each suitor is the same each night, falling asleep moments after dinner."

"For your safety, prince, do not overanalyze the situation." I kept walking.

"How will I protect you if you do not allow me."

"Where you come from maybe you save damsels in distress but here, I do not need protection."

That night the suitor fell asleep in the dining room, my father retired to his chambers and I dismissed Harold from my side. After five days my father was oblivious to the situation, he did not notice the pattern arising and despite trying to be cautious, Harold entered my chamber by force. He was surprised to see me wearing my armor with dual curved swords hanging from my back.

"I sooner say you are having a bad dream for you to leave me be," I said after a moment of silence.

"Emirah, what is going on?"

"You are a foreigner and will not understand."

"Then help me understand."

"I have been drugging each suitor and sneaking out of the palace each day to learn more about the other suitors." Harold looked even more confused than before. I exhaled and explained as best as I was able to, "No one is going to save my kingdom. The nation is corrupt from inside out, and I have to learn what men will not tell a woman. I have to save my nation. I know you are not a threat, that is why you are still here, but I can not let you get involved. Even if

I tried to explain, this situation is unexplainable, so please just do not interfere."

"With all due respect I am here, I have to help."

"Harold, you do not have to be here, there are situations beyond your control."

"I may not understand the politics involved, but what will you gain dressing up like this? By infiltrating the suitors at night, and persuading them with womanly charms in the morning? What happens when there are no suitors left and you have to make a choice?"

"That is a good question, I did not consider that. Besides, why do you care what happens next?"

"Emirah, I do not have to know the history of your kingdom nor the politics in order to understand that my life is at risk by the outcome regardless of what I say, it is not like I will rush and warn your father. I have been here five days and all I see is a man, tired of making choices to the point where he does not act as a ruler, letting the situation unfold before him. Do you take him for a fool for not interfering in the last days? He knows how independent you are and is allowing you to be yourself, but as a father he is not protecting you from the hardest choice that you have to make in the end."

"Why do you even care, as you say, you only have known me for five days?"

"I care because it is my duty to protect you. I am not your father, but if he will not act upon it, then as your custodian I will."

Without saying more, I jumped out of the window. Harold did not follow me, the next day was carried out like the other days before. The tenth day finally arrived and on that morning the thrill of knowing a new person and infiltrating the others to learn more of their hidden intentions vanished, now was the moment to make a decision.

"Noble suitors, I hope that in these last days you rested and were able to befriend my daughter by gaining her trust, all in the hope that one will marry. Now my daughter will announce whom among you will be her husband," my father announced. I stood up and approached the suitors.

"There is a conspirator in our midst. He can reveal himself or I will personally eliminate this potential threat!" I said and there was silence. I began to walk from left to right of the suitors, looking into their eyes.

"Emirah, what is this?" my father raised his voice in shock.

I turned to look and respond, "These men claim to be from royal families, when in truth they belong to a subversive organization."

"Wise sultan, speaking for only myself, I come from Almeida with the noblest of intentions of joining our nations together!" said one of the suitors from the right corner, he stepped forward and from the kneeling position he assumed, he slowly raised his head, finding my father's gaze. A sense of relief came, followed by amusement.

"There is nothing to forgive prince, my daughter is simply postponing the inevitable." my father's visage was full distraught and in shock.

"Do not worry sire, it will be dealt with," the prince said. In one swift, sudden action his right hand reached for a throwing knife hidden inside his vest, and as he rose, his hand released the knife as he stood. The knife flew between my father and I and it stopped in between the eyes of the royal advisor who was standing at the side of my father. Like a statue, he fell with a thump as he hit the ground. My father looked at the dead corpse with his mouth open.

Harold rushed and kicked the prince to the ground, pointing his blade to his throat. "Like your father said, princess Emirah, you are only postponing the inevitable!"

"Your hasty actions caused you to miss your target." I said calmly.

A suitor still in line spoke, "Princes Emirah, you can either choose one of the nine of us whom remain, or the Association will…"

"Will do what exactly?" I did not allow him to finish, I continued, "Your schemes end here. I will not marry one of you only for the rest of you to manipulate my city. Leave now while I still allow you to go with your lives."

The whole room turned to face me. I glanced to my left, and then I reached inside my blue garments pulling out a knife and threw it

64

at one of my father's guards. When he fell, I simply said, "If there are any members of the Association present in this court room, I repeat, leave now while I still allow it!"

"Guards, arrest her!" my father, shocked by my behavior ordered the royal guard to enter the room. I assumed a stance by sliding my left foot backwards while I could still face forwards.

"Father, I know there is confusion at the moment, but once the truth is revealed, all will make sense. But I must remind you that my quarrel is not with thee, but I will defend myself." My father did not heed this warning and neither did the guards for as two men were approaching me, one reached to seize my hands, I swiftly grabbed his hand as my elbow made contact with his face, in the same motion the second attacker grabbed my shoulder. I countered the attack by grabbing the guard by his collar and taking him out by breaking his nose with my forehead.

The room turned into a fighting arena as the remaining nine suitors surrounded me. Very calmly I turned, as the men were moving. As soon as they stopped, I stopped. A long moment passed before one of the guards cried as he rushed with a thrusting movement of his spear. I dodged the thrust and grabbed the spear at the same time. Tilting the spear out of the guard's grip, I turned while at the same time making the guard fall with the butt end of the spear. As he was falling down, the sharp edge penetrated his clothes, nailing him to the ground. As three men now charged, I tuned in a circle to unravel my blue dress to reveal my leather armor and reached for the sword concealed at my back, parrying every blow the men delivered. As one blow was directed to chop of my head, I ducked and in the same motion my sword reached for his ribs. As I pulled my sword, I slashed the neck of the second. The following attack of the third suitor was a counter that made him lose the grip of his sword, throwing it to the air as my agile blade cut his stomach. Before the sword of the fallen suitor was about to hit the floor, I managed to grab its hilt to parry the attack of the fourth and fifth suitors who charged forward but ended up flanking me on each side. This next action seemed synchronized, for as the two men charged at the same time, I calmly stepped aside watching how both pierced each other.

The remaining five charged together, but this time I parried and retreated closer to the throne. Now I was completely surrounded for reinforcements entered the room.

"Brave princess, lay down your sword and I will be merciful with you. Pursue this malice even further and I will break you!" my father spoke with grand authority."

CHAPTER X

꜠ ꜡

Harold then continued the story: Emirah simply responded, "Unfortunately I can't abide to these terms, but I accept the first half our proposal." With this she dropped the sword of the suitor she had acquired earlier and brandished her own sword in a fancy way by realizing her grip and as it was in the air the back of her hand, swung the hilt so the blade was pointing downward to the scabbard. It seemed she was about to surrender, but as she turned, she charged towards where I was standing.

She extended her right hand; in my confusion I extended my left hand, forgetting about the suitor I was overseeing with my sword. She then abducted me and we flew out of the window. I thought this was the end for both of us but we ended up in the royal carriage. The princess embraced me and she absorbed the impact, keeping me out of harm's way. As she positioned herself to drive the carriage, the king poked his head out. I could not tell whether he was now outraged or beyond angry. But her dad with a puzzled voice said, "I thought our proposal was to surrender?'"

"No father, I meant choosing a suitor. Was not that the very first half of our proposal?" Ending her statement by looking at her father, waiting for an answer the chariot drove us away from the palace. I only heard the sultan screaming. I cannot possibly picture what his face looked like. Part of me was afraid for I now stood in the hands of a woman I thought I had never met in my entire life, only knowing her for ten days.

"Can I know what all that was back there?' I said, when I recovered from the fall.

"O Harold, forgive me. Allow me to explain myself." Emirah responded courteously.

"You'd better! After all, not only did you anger your father, but you abducted me. Not to mention it is I who decides whether to marry or not." When we rode out of the main gates of the city an arrow pierced the side of the carriage. There was an archer following us and he kept shooting. My heart began to beat uncontrollably.

She halted the carriage and said, "Be quick about it, for I am going with my betrothed to his kingdom."

'The Sultan demands the return of the princess, as her custodian you are charged to return her, prince Harold," said the man.

'Tell my father, the sultan, that I will return but first I will seek the means to save the nation.'

"You leave me with no choice princess, I will bring you back, even if I have to harm you in the process," he said, aiming an arrow.

"Before you loose the arrow, know that as her custodian I will defend the princess before anything else, and you are threatening her." I said.

"Prince, you are in a hard situation, she claims you are her future husband yet you have not acquired her father's blessing, and your duty lies with him, help me bring her back."

"My duty is to watch over her, I go where she goes, yours rest with the sultan and thus will return empty handed. As warriors let our blades decide whose duty shall prevail, for I will not comply with you and you have to go through me in order to acquire the princess."

He lowered the bow, unmounted the horse, and drew out his curved sword. I approached to close the distance as I did, he was the first to strike, thrusting at my neck; I parried and made a thrust so to penetrate his armor. With the hilt of his blade he lowered my thrust and intended to hit me with the hilt. I used the hilt of my blade to lower his and in a swift motion he punched me, releasing our blades. He charged to cut sideways, but using my blade from the edge I used the hilt to parry and punched him in the chest with the hilt, as he stepped back, I grabbed the blade from the hilt and prepared an upper cut when the call to prayer echoed across the city.

Emirah descended from the chariot and kneeled to pray. I looked at the soldier, lowered my guard and said, "Go ahead and pray, our quarrel can wait."

"At this moment my duty comes before prayer." He charged and our blades clashed. He then swung for my head, I lowered my body stepping in front of the swing and behind him, in the same motion I cut his legs behind the knees. Once on the ground, I pushed aside his blade.

"Defend the sultan, for there is more that you yet do not understand. Tell him that I will return with his daughter." As I began to walk to the carriage, Emirah was standing behind the carriage, holding to the edge. She walked in front of the horses and I heard her say:

Brave and noble knight
Defend thy kings pride
From the melees of the night.

Like the braking dawn,
Become the pawn of hope
That will return glory
To our king's home.

Your luster sparks a beam of light
Upon the twilight of the dark

At the hour of fight,
Confront and shatter thy enemies.
Decimate, but never forget thy virtue.

For thy brave words strike fear
Upon your fallen foes,
As you annunciate these words:

'Be gone and admit your honorable defeat
For next time we meet,
My sword shall speak for me.'

I then had the urge to say, "This will sound strange, but you seem familiar somehow. Have we met before?"

"Well as you may know, Europe and the Middle East have been at war and our marriage could provide peace, by showing an alternative to fighting. However, on the course of the ten days I learned as much as I was able to, regarding the Association. As soon as I married they would kill my father and remove themselves from the rule of Saladin. As for how we know each other..."

There was a very long pause before my eyes recognized Emirah, for she annunciated something I said a long time ago, "Flower of beauty, please be the joy of my heart." These words echoed with familiarity! She continued, "These words I heard from this very man two years ago while shopping in a European town. At first, he wanted to sell me something, but he ended up flattering me before we departed with those same words. Every day since then I felt I had found someone who valued me for who I was, instead of the wealth of a princess or the power of my father." She stepped closer to me and continued, "You risked your life in a daring mission to be my custodian not knowing who I was, and held true to your duty as you have shown me. Now I wonder if you will defend me, and my nation now that your heart recognizes me?"

"Emirah with your love I'll never be alone." As we got closer she embraced me and for the very first time our lips were sealed as we rode out to the sunset.

The challenges we are going through to get married, is a story in the process. I need the courage to ask my father to send soldiers to help the city of Emirah and my brother will not pick up a sword to aid me in my crusade," Harold concluded their tale.

CHAPTER XI

❧❧

N ow Gerald stepped in, "Well brother, let me share with you my
circumstance:

Two years ago, when we took separate roads after our venture in
the enchanted palace with Yrian, I decided to go back home and ask
father for a small piece of land from my inheritance to be a wood-
cutter. He questioned me, and I responded, "I shall learn modesty,
and to value what is given to me, if one day I will inherit the responsibilities of our kingdom, hence I shall provide firewood for the
settlements of our kingdom and ask for nothing in return."

My father applauded my intentions and gave me his blessing.
Each morning I took my axe and had to distinguish between log-
ging healthy trees and those that no longer bloomed. I carried out
this lifestyle for one year until one day an old lady approached me
and said, "I am hungry, can you give me some food?"

"I only have a piece of bread, but gladly I shall share it with you."

"You have a gentle heart," she said, and we sat below the shadow
of a tree to eat. Afterwards she said, "I have been looking for a person such as you to help me to accomplish an important task." She
then explained, "Follow this road, not far from here you will find
an old oak tree. In one of its branches hangs a fine red cape. Seven

black hawks guard it; only one has a red feather. Climb the tree, pluck out the red feather, once they fly away, bring me the cape."

"I will accomplish such a simple task with ease," I said and followed the path she showed me. Indeed, the oak was not far; there were the cape and the wild hawks, but they did not intimidate me. I climbed with ease and approached the hawks, despite their unfriendly appearance, and to my surprise, they did not rush to attack me. I plucked out the red feather and the hawks flew in disarray. I took the cape and the branch was no longer able to support my weight and cracked. I landed hard on the ground but remained unscathed.

When I gave the old lady the garment she said, "This is no ordinary cape, it is magical. Wear it and it will take you to whichever place you desire."

I looked at her, confused, "Why shall I need a magic cape?"

She wrapped the cape around my shoulders saying, "An evil warlock captured princes Flora, and locked her in a tower because she refuses to marry him. You will be able to rescue her with the magic of this cape." Before I was able to reply she warned me, "The warlock Malgar is quite incisive," and vanished.

"I must be dreaming, I said, "while it lasts, I will play along." I closed my eyes and tested if the cape was really magical. I wished to be in my chamber room, in the castle of my father, and instantly I was in the castle and far from my cabin in the woods.

'This cape is truly magical!' I exclaimed in amusement. My reinvigoration to set out on adventures such as when I was young rushed through my body, and I decided to save this princess.

I wished to be in the market, where I proceeded to inquire to learn where to find princess Flora. I traveled quickly from one kingdom to another across Europe to find her and finally I found where she was held captive, in the region where Yrian came from. When I was outside her castle, I saw a glimpse of princess Flora, "She is very beautiful, but she looks sad," I observed.

Meanwhile the evil warlock Malgar was inside the castle, peering into his crystal ball. When he saw Gerald wearing the cape, the orb reflected his perverse smile and said, "That old witch gave this stranger the red cape so he could rescue the princess, but I shall take it from him."

When I knocked on the door, Malgar opened and stood to welcome me.

"Is it possible for me to spend the night here?"

"Of course lad, come in," he said with an Irish accent, he looked old with a long pointy nose with a large mole, big eyebrows, and a red beard. His robe and wizard hat were purple.

He led me to the dining room and brought me a plate full of food. While eating from a turkey leg, I said with my mouth open, "Who is the princess I saw in the top of the tower?"

"Princess? There are no princess here, I am sure you were having a vision."

"Ah!" I swallowed my food, took a sip of wine, tore another bite of the turkey leg and said, "Visions, such as the one you have, court wizard? I do not think I have developed such skills as of now!"

Malgar began to walk away from the dining room but turned his glance to say, "I must ask that you do not leave the room, when I return we can discuss these visions and talk to ghosts if it shall amuse you."

There was no fooling him, but once he left I rushed to hide the cape inside a set of armor that decorated the room. This one had the insignia of a falcon on the right, a vertical yellow stripe, and a hand on the left. Then I opened the door leading to the main hall, glanced from right to left, and back again, and there was no one in sight. I left the dining room, muffling each step. To my ears came a sobbing weep, following the sound I found the stairs that lead up to the tower, I ascended to find Flora. At the end of the stairway there was a locked door.

A lid opened, revealing the visage of the princess. "Please do not cry. I am here to rescue you," I bravely tried to console her.

"How will you rescue me if the door is locked?"

"Do not worry, I have a magical cape that will help." I then rushed down the stairs and back to the dining room to get the cape. It took longer to reach the dining room and I fell asleep in the first room I found. I did not suspect that the evil Malgar had scattered a magic dust that causes sleep. The warlock found my cape and replaced it with a similar one. When I woke from the magic slumber I realized how late it was and rushed to find the cape. Without wasting more time, I returned to the princess.

"Quick! Put the cape on and wish to be outside with me!"

Flora placed the cape around her, closed her eyes, and wished hard but nothing happened.

"Wish it with all your might!" I suggested, peeping through the lid with a smile.

"I am wishing to be far away from here as possible and nothing is happening!" she exclaimed.

"Perhaps the cape is broken," I said with an embarrassed expression.

To make matters worse, I heard footsteps climbing the stairs. I looked around and hid myself inside a barrel that stood outside the door.

Malgar then opened the door and in a thundering voice shouted with his hands extended, showing the real cape, "So you tried to escape, princess. Do you know what happened? I took the real enchanted cape and this peasant will not be able to rescue you! Now you shall marry me!"

"Not even in your dreams, crazy old man!" she shouted, matching his voice and extending her face towards his.

Her reply simply infuriated him; he began to wave his wand around her and turned her into an ugly frog. Malgar closed his eyes, placed both hands on his chest and laughed hysterically. He then bended so to look at the eyes of the frog saying, "Lo! This is the end of the stubborn princess!"

At this I came out of hiding and in trying to understand the situation I questioned, "What did you do to her?"

Malgar simply turned around, no longer with a smile but and evil grin and waved his wand. I was unaware of what happened, but I appeared in the forest. I looked around, there was my axe, the lumber I was cutting, and it was midday. I simply rolled my eyes saying, "What a dream…"

"A dream where you find an old lady, a magical cape, travel to a kingdom ruled by an evil warlock who wants to marry a princess who is now a frog?" I turned around and there stood the old lady. With my eyes wide I simply extended my legs and dropped to the floor, resting my back on a tree and exclaimed, "Malgar tricked me!"

"Do not worry, we will help the princess."

I stood up, wiped away the leaves about me and demanded, "First tell me who you are and why are you so interested in saving her, why not do it yourself?"

"I believe I owe you as much, Flora never knew her parents. Her mother died giving birth to her and her father was cursed. I took it upon myself to raise her, but she has grown independent, not listening to my counsel. I know who you are Gerald, you can save her from Malgar—the counselor of his father who brought about all the demise of the family, and show Flora who you truly are, a prince worthy of her, and to preserve her kingdom." She stood before me and from her satchel revealed two colored cabbages saying, "These are…"

"Let me guess, magic cabbages," I replied.

She ignored my lack of enthusiasm to carry on, lifted me and dressed me in old clothing to make me look like a beggar. She reveled the secret of the cabbages and concluded, "Now close your eyes, rub your nose, and you shall be outside the palace."

Instead of knocking I set up a shop outside the castle and began to shout loudly, "Magic cabbages for sale! Come buy your magic cabbages! Or just give a coin for a poor beggar, but do not miss the chance to buy magic cabbages!" I did so until nightfall, and at first glimmer of light of the next day I continued yelling and rambling on and on about the cabbages.

"What do you want, ragged beggar?" Malgar walked out of the palace, annoyed.

"I bring these magic cabbages!" I then extended the red cabbage saying, "I will offer you a free sample and you will see that something wonderful shall occur!"

"Bah! There is no such a thing as magic cabbages, but only if it will get you to stop with your rambling, I shall try." Soon after swallowing a single bite, Malgar transformed into a donkey! I left him whining hysterically and climbed up the tower. I stood before the enchanted frog and gave her the green cabbage.

Then and there she was, transformed and returned to her former self, saying, "Oh you are my hero! How shall I reward you?"

"It is time I reveal who I really am, I am prince Gerald of the kingdom of Mercia, just grant me time to better know you in hope that it will serve you in a greater way."

She embraced me and in joy exclaimed, "Every girl wishes for a brave prince to sweep her off her feet, and here is one who came to save me in my time of need!"

That same day she announced our marriage and instructed to proceed with all preparations. In the course of the year there were delays, this caused Flora to become impatient and instead threw out parties and ignored the responsibilities to her kingdom.

Each night, I saw her talking to other men and one day I confronted her saying, "Flora stop celebrating in this manner, there is more to be a princess than to socialize and celebrate."

"What is the problem in knowing other wealthy and powerful men? This sort of life is about connections Gerald."

"Do not fool me Flora! If you wish to make alliances so be it, but do not ignore my affections towards you!"

"You think that only because you saved me from that old and ugly looking warlock you are my fiancé? You are no different from him in that case. I am free to choose whom I please," she responded in a calm and unworried manner.

"All you do is use your womanly charms and status as princess and enjoy how men flock around you!" shouted a drunken voice. Standing at our side was a man holding a cup of wine.

"Robert? What are you doing here?"

"I am," he began to take steps to stand closer to us, but the wine had consumed him and his balance was out of alignment. "I have finally mustered the courage to tell you who you really are. And who is this?" He signaled at me with both hands, he took a sip of wine, and after hiccup said, "Do not tell me, your new bachelor, falling for you and your ploy."

"Robert stop embarrassing yourself, what we had was nice, but you are not the one for me. I soon realized it was best to remain friends and have strong connections with our nations."

"Do all your connections kiss you and promise to love you in sacred matrimony only for you to change your mind? At this rate I am amused none of them see you for who you really are, a hag!"

"Robert how dare you insult me! Apologize now!"

To this the drunken man lifted his hands and began to say:

A shining sun illuminates a forest like a town;
from afar a melody brings me to life!
I now see a maid with dark brown hair.
Her charming voice echoes through in a rife.

I follow her path, as more creatures come to her praise.
I feel like Odysseus, entranced by the siren's song.
Approaching to meet her, we enter a new phase.

I dare not depart to stay and talk with thee,
but time moves along.
She says adieu; for I will not see her once more.
My feelings beckon me to go to her.
Wait too long, she will walk through the door.
Rushing to her, I grab what strength is left and confer.

Letting my emotions flow,
Hoping she will glow.

He ended by embracing Flora, her eyes in a sea of doubt but before she was able to say anything Robert dropped to the ground, consumed by the wine. In his place now stood the warlock Malgar with fiery eyes that matched the color of his hair, standing in the entrance of the hall—what remained was lighting flashing around him with thunder announcing his entrance. The wizard exclaimed with a moderate tone of voice saying, "This is the end, princess. First, I transform you into an old hag so that you may learn the value of beauty, then into a frog so you may know what it is to be ugly. Now comes despair, and loss, and shame."

"What sorrows do you speak of Malgar?" said a new voice, belonging to the old lady. She continued saying, "The sort that engulfs your world?"

"Oh, you witch! This night becomes even better. I can take my revenge on the two of you once and for all!"

"Do not harm Flora," said the old lady of the forest. "Your quarrel is with me!" she challenged.

"Harm is far too gentle for her. Flora shall remain awake and still, without the ability to speak for herself in this very place, where she now stands, until a man who truly loves her proclaims true and honest feelings of devotion for her. And only when she weeps tears of sadness, in recognition of her own folly, then, and only then will she be released!"

Flora moved her eyes and mouth but was not able to speak or move anything else. Malgar then waved his wand around Robert who stood up, sober by a new enchantment. Malgar then signaled Robert to approach Flora saying, "Go ahead, and proclaim your love for Flora." As if hypnotized Robert approached and said all he felt for her, but she did not move.

"This is what you deserve for not valuing what is in front of you," and Robert walked away.

One man approached her saying, "Flora, it is me Trisian, I always had feelings for you when we were young, and I finally want to share them with you." Nothing happened, Trisian lowered his head, then rose, kissed her in the forehead and said, "I hope one day you return to your former self." He left and soon all who listened gathered in the party simply began to walk away until only Malgar, the old lady, and I were left.

"Go on, tell Flora what you feel Gerald,'" Malgar signaled me to approach her.

"I told Flora all I needed to say before you worked your magic," I said. I do not know if my inaction was of bravery or if I did not want to get involved with the trickster.

"Malgar," the old lady said, caressing Flora. "I am truly displeased with you. I hate you so, hopefully when love runs over you, it hits you with joy for you to faint from laughter as you explode with happiness, and ultimately for God to shower you with blessings."

"Do not speak of love, for you brought more harm to her than I ever did! All I am doing is to show her what love really is."

"What is love to you Malgar?" she asked, standing up to face him.

He began to walk closer to her and said, "You know very well what love is, nothing but a sickness that consumes king and peasant alike, with nothing but lust, and for this malady people will kill and die for a feeling they can not understand."

"Malgar, you were not like this, once you were a wise man."

"Who was consumed by love, and I rose out of its murky shadow to see the truth!"

"Malgar, what did I ever do to you for you to curse an innocent child?"

"What did you do to me? O, she has the nerve to ask!"

"I am opening myself to you Malgar, I am willing to abandon our rivalry, but just for one moment at least try not to utter harmful phrases or use your magic to harm others."

"Listen to yourself, it is the guilt and the sorry you feel towards me that is making you weak. Where is the enchantress that once rivaled me and stole my secrets?"

"Malgar, if I ever wronged you, I am here now, but please don't unleash what you feel on others."

"Once I was in love and saw the treachery of your womanly ways. When my king suffered at the hands of love, time after time, as if cursed from ever being next to a woman, I saved him."

"By letting a baby girl grow in absence of her father? Malgar, please! Just listen to yourself!"

"It is too late now. Once a spell is cast, it can not be undone."

"Why are you punishing Flora for trying to find her way in the world?"

"Your attempts fail to resonate with me. I told you, I have grown stronger, you mean nothing to me."

"It is clear that your words have poisoned your heart."

Without saying more, Malgar disappeared. I then approached Flora and the old lady. "You said I was going to help, but it seems I am just a pawn in the game of two wizards."

"You did help Gerald, more than you think. I see clearly now."

"Whatever there is between the two of you I am now part of this, and I want to see Flora safe," I said looking into her eyes.

"Thank you, Gerald," she embraced me. "A magician always needs the strength of a warrior to take action, and your words lift me to see her safe as well."

"Do not thank me yet, only when this is over. What shall we do?"

She grabbed me and pulled me aside from Flora, then said so only I could hear, "The spell Malgar casted upon her may refer to her father. If only we can find him, if he is still alive, he may be able to lift the spell."

"There is no greater love than a father's love for a child. Only he can inflict those emotions when she looks at him," I said, and she then nodded in agreement.

"Very well, but first let me gather my thoughts, I shall look for you when I am ready, and have discovered the location of her father so I can travel to his location quickly with the cape," I concluded and she handed me the magical cape. I walked towards Flora, gently wrapped both my palms in one of hers and said, "Soon, all will be back to normal, do not worry, I will help you once again not because of the previous promise when I last saved you, but because I wish to see you well." I kissed her on the forehead and left.

Gerald concluded his tale, and everyone was silent, until he continued: "Now we are here Yrian, to ask for your help once again."

CHAPTER XII

ಌ⬩ಌ

"H ow can I help you?" I asked, confused.
Gerald leaned closer to me and said, "When we entered the enchanted palace two years ago, you saved the king, and you remained in his company. I have reason to believe he is Flora's father."

"We dare not ask for his help Yrian," said Harold. "It is proper you ask him, because by helping my eldest brother I can ask my father to give me his blessing to marry Emirah and with the small force of his soldiers we can set out to save her kingdom."

"Harold wait, I never said I would marry Flora once she is free from the spell!" remarked Gerald impatiently.

"Let me get this straight, do you, Harold, love Emirah or do you simply want to grow your name and kingdom? And you, Gerald, what is your purpose in helping Flora?" Junichi was sitting in an unusual kneeling position he called seiza, with his eyes facing the fire, then slightly raised his expression to find Harold's.

Harold was silent and Gerald after a moment said, "I do not know if I should even save her, yet I do, and still don't know why I have feelings for her, but it is all in a cloud of confusion. She is childish, and why should I be the one to save her? In the end she is likely to leave me for the next handsome prince that comes along

83

her way. Why do men have to venture far and wide only to appease women? We fight wars, we protect them, and what do they do? I do not deserve this, I was content in my cabin until I was dragged into this." He turned his head, held it with both hands and lowered his head between his legs saying, "Why are women so complicated?"

"You think men have it hard boy, and you ask what women do?" remarked Junichi in a tone I'd never heard before. "Let me tell you, they bleed and weep, giving men, and particularly kings, the only thing that matters to them: an heir to look after their wealth once they are gone!"

"Finally, a man that understands," Emirah said without thinking.

"Everyone please," I stepped in, placed my left hand on Gerald's shoulder saying, "You and your brother have grown from adolescent boys to men, I see you very differently today. Gerald, you came here for a reason, finish what you promised not for her, but because you can be the hero you wanted to be when I first met you. If she truly values you, she will see you for who you really are, just as you see her for who she really is, not to diminish her, but lift her up from the murky corners of her mind to a bright world!"

"Yrian do not encourage him to fight for love," Junichi said.

I stood up and responded, "Junichi only because you do not believe in love, does not mean others have to overcome that emotion and repress it," I paused and he looked at me silently. "I am sorry if this situation makes you uncomfortable I know your story and I do not want to hurt you."

"I am the one who should apologize," Junichi stood up, "Emirah and Harold, enjoy and treasure what you have," he addressed them by placing one hand on each of their shoulders. "You are young and open with your emotions and deserve one another, may your crusade save your nation." Junichi then looked at the eldest brother, looking into his green eyes saying, "As for you Gerald, I hope you succeed in your quest."

I then told my trusted friend, "You were once a great warrior, come with us, perhaps witnessing how this story plays out will help you."

"The invigoration to set out on a quest died with the samurai I left in Japan. Go, I will look after the farm."

"Let us rest, for tomorrow we shall journey back to the enchanted palace and reunite the monarch with his lost daughter."

"Yrian use the magic cape, we shall meet you and the monarch where Flora is," said Gerald, offering me the cape. I took it and did not hesitate to travel to the enchanted palace.

One moment I was on my farm, the next in the lake where the duck helped me to find the key. Looking at the water reflecting on the moonlight caused me to get lost in a drain of consciousness. I decided to wait until morning and slept against the closest tree.

That morning I entered the palace. Even without the spell that transformed all into stone, the palace still seemed absent of color and life. The torches and chandeliers did not light the halls, and the only sound was a lament. It was the voice of the king, saying:

Dark Specters that crawl
Shading the path ahead
Absence of the light, why can't I see beyond?

It must be because you can't brawl.
Dead phantom that never flees
From what murky darkness thou has spawned?

Out of the welcoming twilight,
The immense shadow of nigh comes forth.
Darkness brings the incubus evil
That flies and hides away.

Away...away...away...
But I fail to see beyond,
For the nigh blinds my sigh again.

At day shadows crawl;

Darkness falls, and they are ever present!
Horrible, terrible, devastating!
Is all I think, for it taunts me upon the hour of midnight.
Asleep I fall, only to be embraced by thy murky grasp.

I opened the door where the noise came from and there stood the monarch with an unhealthy appearance: old sleeping garments tarnished by the absence of being removed, a long grey beard and unwashed hair, and his sleepless eyes looking beyond the window. I stood next to him; he did not seem to notice my presence. I said to him, "What do you see?"

"A world absent of love."

"Do you remember me my king?" I asked, turning my head to find his eyes. He simply turned and nodded then looked back at the forest, the sky and clouds of a beautiful morning, to my eyes, but not his.

"I remember when you told me your tragic story, I have reason to believe I can help you out of the misery you find yourself in right now."

He then walked away from the window and slowly walked about the room, waving his arms, holding his chest, and expressing the following words:

"An empty feeling like the void overshadows my heart and thoughts. No sun, no supernova, can brighten this feeling, for I am haunted by my past memories and events.

Owl that hoots the woe of night, no wisdom can I find but only the sorrow found in a deep scorn of hollow. The grief you cause, I can only swallow. Having to regret the murky path I now follow.

That pain aches with every breath I take. That pain hurts with every heartbeat. That pain yearns with suffering with the passing of time. That pain is— the languish of my tormented grief.

I beg a thief to steal my bitter condolence away! I plead with all my might for healing! Determined I try to forget! With no result I kneel before my shameful defeat. Recovery. Recovery. Recovery...is the echo to which I pray. For the further away it goes, my hopes turn to despair.

This broken-heartedness; is a wound that I will never fully heal. No elixir, no doctor, no medicine, no antibiotic, no drug, no prayer can avail me from my scourge. For my nemesis is like an agonizing bane.

This burden...I can carry no further. How long must I suffer? So come what sorrow can, for now I sleep, only to awake and feel this vacuum void once again."

He concluded, sitting in the edge of the bed. I sat next to him and asked, "For whom do you weep my lord, for wife who died, or a child you never knew?"

"I do not know." He covered his face with his palms crying, holding his head between his legs.

I placed my left hand over to his left side and with my free hand I consoled him. A moment later I said, "There is a world beyond these hollow walls, just listen to what I have to say."

"Ah, Yrian," the monarch wiped his tears away, regained his posture then continued, "I think my grief was never like this when I was a gnome."

"No my lord, in being human again, you are now expressing sadness, something you probably hid and tried to forget as a gnome." I halted, for I did find the wording to mention Flora. Finally I said, "Now use whatever you feel as motivation to find what you have lost, for I know where your daughter is."

The monarch turned to find my eyes and stood up saying, "That is not possible!"

"It may not be possible yes, there is no guarantee for there is a young princess by the name of Flora who has been trapped by a spell that only words of true love can set her free. She may not be your daughter my king, but channel your emotions as if she were your daughter and save her."

"Yes." The king stood up, "YES!" he repeated, "There may not be any challenges for an old man like me to face, nor villains to slay, but this is certainly something I will gladly do!" Invigorated, the monarch tore off his wrinkly old shirt and to my surprise, despite his old age, his muscles seemed rather strong. "Give me a moment, let me find my old armor." Then he appeared clad in a dark suit of armor from helm to foot, as the night itself. "Two years ago, you drew out the king inside me, now you have revived the Ebony Knight—that is what they used to call me."

CHAPTER XIII

⟿ ⟾

When I began to walk out of the palace I spotted a bird across the portcullis in a tree. It flew right away; I froze, following its flight across the sky. The bird was similar to Portia's, with black-feathered wings and a red belly. The king rode out on his black stallion and asked me why I stopped, coming out of my trance I said, "Nothing, I lost focus, let us continue." I mounted the brown horse he had for me and galloped beyond the forest to reach Flora.

The reason I did not offer the warrior king the ability to use the cape was so that the journey to save Flora held deeper meaning. In fact, I had difficulty matching the speed of his stallion. Crossing the forest, the region where my farm was, the town where I had worked with John in the mill, and finally coming back to the palace where Flora was may seem that all was in proximity, but I assure you, one's perception of distance varies on the urgency of the movement. When I first ventured in the forest, when I first meet Harold and Gerald, our adventure in the forest lasted three days until we found the enchanted palace. When I first found Flora, as an old lady in a distant part of the same woods, that anecdote took me a day and a half. To tell you the truth, the magic of the forest extended beyond time and space, finally brought us all together.

When the king and I reached at the palace after riding for one day, arriving at night, we entered the palace where Flora stood in company of Harold, Emirah, Gerald, and the old lady.

"Rachel, is it really you?" the king asked the old lady, removing his dark helm.

"It is my king, I am glad to see you after all these years."

"Those years have been kind to you...unlike me."

"Save those emotions for one who needs it most," Rachel said then stepped closer, holding the king by one had and extending the other saying, "Look who stands before you."

The king began to move slowly not because of the weight of his armor, but at the surprise. When he was in front of Flora he said, "I recognize that smile and those eyes. The visage of the one person who truly recognized me, who valued me, and granted me the love I longed for during all my youth."

Flora stood with her left hand extended, her palm facing up; the king grasped her hand gently with his right hand and continued, "Dear Flora, you are now the same age when I first meet your mother. I held you when you were born, thanking your mother, comforting her, telling her that her efforts had not been in vain, that you were safe, surrounded by love. Only for her to pull me close saying, 'I am sorry I have to leave you...I am no different than the others that came before me.' Before I was able to say more, she died."

The king closed his eyes, dropping his helm making a loud clank on the floor. He fell on his knees, still holding on to her hand, "All my life, love has been torment and grief." He began to weep; he then let go of her hand to support his body, the weight of his heart was heavier than his armor. After a moment, he embraced Flora from her legs.

When he was finally able to speak again he stood up and looked at Flora in the eyes saying, "I was devastated at the sight of her dying that without care, I dropped you on the bed, next to her and left the room to regain my thoughts. I was a coward for disregarding you. You are not to blame my child. Your mother was sick before giving birth to you. I never blamed you, but abandoned you for not facing my situation. Rachel was there, encouraging me to hold you and be with you, but the torment of her passing consumed me. Know that I always loved you, Flora, from the moment you were born, but lacked the necessary love to nourish you. But I am here, take pity on this old man, let me be the father you need to guide you in the time that we may have together, for how ever short or long it may last."

He embraced her, and she closed both eyes and tears began to run down her eyes, the spell was lifted and she was able to move and speak, saying, "Why did you leave me?" Flora's voice was finally heard across the hall, and she was able to wrap her arms around his father for the first time in her life.

With his eyes closed, when he felt her embrace the king stood up, spinning around with her with a smile and in laugher lifted her up, "Even at my old age, I can lift you as the first day you were born." He lowered her gently, with an embrace he said, "I ran away because I did not want you to feed off of my misery. I was afraid because I did not know how to love you." He once again looked at her while holding her shoulders saying, "Will you grant me permission to be your father, and learn to love you?"

Before she was able to respond, there was a loud clapping, we all turned and, in the entrance, stood Malgar with his sinister smile, after having our attention he said, "Is this not a lovely reunion?"

"You took everything from me with your leech craft!" said the king.

"Wait, as I recall you wanted to surpass your grief, to look fierce in the face of your enemies, and now here he stands at last! How did the bards sing of your grandiosity?" Malgar crossed his arms, looking away for the answer, then extended his arms and recited:

There be a tale of the grand soldier of twilight,
Who wields the forces of night and day.
Whose valor illuminates bright
With sundown glimmer that springs away.

Knight of chivalry, ride onward to the sun, where it sets,
To set forth a ritual to summon thee at the Luster Shrine.
With courage, open the gates of chaos, do not forget,
For the forces of light and darkness now intertwine.

The envoy of the beginning emerges from chaos,
For he is the emissary of good and evil,
Who battles doubt with his sword and shield of pathos.
Yet, his courage to strive in turmoil is thy upheaval.

Your is might shining murkiness,
Thou art the Obscure soldier of Lightness.

The king held Flora tight, and remained silent. After a moment Malgar continued, "You sought to be strong in the face of your enemies, and to overcome your grief."

"Your remedy made me a nightmare to all, look at the dark armor you cursed!"

"And yet you wear it."

"I am not afraid of admitting who I truly am."

"You were destined for greatness my king, but then you found this…" Malgar pointed at Rachel, when he finally found the word said, "This witch, so you could escape from your true nature!"

"With your counsel I would have become a horrible king! Ruling with an iron fist, enslaving my enemies who did not share your views, and when I needed your counsel in matters of the heart, I failed time and time again."

Malgar pointed at the king saying, "That is not true!" He lowered his finger, and his expression away, then moved his eyes back to the king saying, "I saved you from the torment."

"Be that as it may! I am not here to discuss how I became a gnome and my kingdom to stone, or who I was in times past, I am here for my daughter to be a new man; not a warrior, nor a king, but a father."

"No one escapes from whom they really are. You will always be a heartless man who will die alone."

"Stop speaking, Flora is free from your spell, so am I! Whatever you want, just please, leave us be."

"Let's show your daughter who you really are, and see if she agrees to be with you."

Then the shade of a woman appeared saying, "O king! I am your flower! I weep because you destroyed my village."

"Collateral damage, I was a fool to think you would marry me after you saw me kill your brother in the battlefield."

A new shade appeared saying, "I am an extinct mermaid! You decimated my race!"

The king began to mumble, and then said, "Out of anger of un-requited love, I order a Viking horde to hunt you down."

"Do not make me choose between my heart and my mind, O, King!" A new shade said.

The king did not dare see the shade, but replied, "On my crusade in Jerusalem I truly fell in love with you, I truly conflicted you with my unworthy love, but never deserved you! I was not clean of my guilt and sins! I asked the Jinn of the Mystic Lamp to force your heart, for you to be be mine! I acknowledge my guilt and leave you in peace."

Shade upon shade appeared, some that I discerned from his old tale, others he did not mention, but a darker truth to the king was revealed. Suddenly a white shade appeared saying, "My king! I love you and accept you for who you are!"

Before seeing this white shade, the king appeared he was about to fall again on his knees and weep, but upon hearing those sweet gentle words the king began to walk towards Malgar. Once in front of him he pushed him with a shield bash saying, "Lo, and behold Malgar! The shade of my wife who does not torment me! You see, I accept who I am, now will you tell us who advised me all those years? I was the one who committed many atrocities, and you must be free of charge because you never lifted a sword to act on behalf of your counsel?"

On the ground Malgar made a gesture with his hand and from it the shadow of the king emerged from the floor to challenge the king. "If so transformed you are then overcome, or be consumed by your own repression!"

The king began to battle his shade, striking and the shadow mirrored all his movements. This was carried on and Malgar laughed and watched in amusement. Until the king lowered his guard, the shadow did not strike, he turned around giving his back to the shadow, placed his blade in the scabbard, took Flora's hand and began to walk away saying, "I will not play your games only because you deny your true self and enjoy taking it out on others."

Malgar cast a fireball to the unsuspecting king, but he blocked it with his shield. The king rushed and choked Malgar saying, "Stop using others for your own amusement! Stop harassing my child to teach her lessons on the real world when you yourself do not live in it! My mercy and generosity have limits, next time I will not hesitate to strike you down!" The king let go and after a brief moment said, "You have lost everything, your credibility, the only friend you had, and the world around you is transforming in the opposite way you envisioned, what happened to the counselor and friend I once had?"

Rachel stood between the king and Malgar. She faced the red bearded warlock saying, "Malgar you have not lost everything, I am here. It is not late to make things right." He simply looked away, down at the floor.

She stood next to him saying, "I am sorry, I stole your alchemy potion—your life's work."

"To use it on a tree!" Malgar shouted, infuriated in his expression, "You wasted my elixir of life, a formula that can not be replicated and you used it on a stupid plant!"

"Malgar, I do not blame you for burning down my secret garden, for leaving me alone on the altar the day we were to be married. You have your reasons, but do not repress your emotions and lash out on those who do not deserve it."

"Why do you even care? It is too late for me Rachel."

"It is never late, I do not see a hideous old warlock but rather..."

"Who I really am?" Malgar mocked her, and then changed his tone of voice, "Rachel stop fooling yourself by love."

"I am the only one here who does not want to either kill you or make you disappear for tormenting their lives! You are far from perfect but so is life, and if you want to be a lonely hermit because no one will dare approach you then so be it!" she began to walk away.

Rachel passed Malgar and before she walked out of the main entrance he turned around and said, "Rachel wait!" She halted and turned to face him, he continued, "The day we were to be married I burned down your garden because you stole my secret formula, but I never harmed that tree—the same tree we planted together. My confusing thoughts about you, that you used me to acquire my work, what you sought with me, ideas of manipulation turned to rage so I destroyed your garden, but I was unable to grab the tree when it was a helpless plant and tore it from the ground root and all."

Then Rachel walked to be in front of Malgar and she asked, "What happened to the tree?"

Malgar began to ponder and eventually said, "I gently put it on a pot and stole it, and in its place, I left a torn plant. I wanted to hurt you." Malgar began to take deep breaths and shortly after continued, "Perhaps I can not make amends, nor make things right, but I will like to show you how big the tree has grown. I do not know why I looked after it through all these years."

She embraced Malgar saying, "I will like to see the tree, lead the way."

"First I have something to say," Malgar walked towards Flora and told her, "Princess, I am sorry I tried to force you to marry me, I tried to show you a dark world, but with your father, and this young man who selflessly saved you a second time, together fight for the world as it should be, may you be blessed for the rest of your days." Malgar then looked at the king and said, "I am sorry for the hardships I made you go through, a path that lead you to escape your pain. I should have counseled you when you needed me most, take care old friend."

"There is nothing to forgive, let us live the rest of our days with joy!" The king embraced Malgar. Afterwards the red bearded magician walked towards Rachel, he embraced her and together began to walk away, he said, "I tried to use my formula to extend my life, but my ambition will now be a gift to vegetation, as the tree is sprouting and its seeds will be able to bring vitality to areas that have been damaged by deforestation." The two walked away from the palace holding each other's hand. Malgar lived with Rachel a more cheerful life by renewing the forest and using his charisma and persuasion to work against deforestation.

The king watched over her daughter and became a true father, guiding her and teaching her how to rule a kingdom. Gerald remained at her side until he traveled to Mercia with her and asked his father to bless them. Harold on the same day received his blessing and the support of the army to help Emirah and her nation of Aljusen.

CHAPTER XIV

W hen I returned to my farm Junichi was troubled and I asked
him what was on his mind, "The other day when I went to
town, I overheard the Dutch merchants say that the Shogun warlord
of Japan had died of natural causes and that his daughter would
take his place."

"Junichi that is great news! Riko may still be alive!"

"Rumors Yrian, nothing more."

"Junichi, the only thing that prevented you from returning home
was the Shogun, he is now gone, and even if Riko is alive or not, I
urge you to rekindle your warrior spirit:

> Age has made you weary
> sweating tears of fatigue,
> draining your spirit away.
> The moment has come to rise.
> Look behind the trail you left,
> others will follow and shout
> with exclamation
> cheering the accomplishment
> you have set forth.

Look at the work and rejoice.
A new horizon awaits for you.

Junichi was staring this whole time at the dirt, when I finished he grasped my shoulder, looked at me and said, "One day kings and peasants will travel far and wide so to heed your counsel in matters of the heart." He handed me the shovel he was holding and continued, "I better catch the vessel before it sets sail."

"Safe travels Junichi." We embraced and I saw him walk away from my farm not looking back, he arrived to the port and to his surprise saw Captain Theunis on the dock.

"Excuse me captain, will you grant me passage to Japan?" Junichi asked.

"Well, well if it isn't the same Jap who five years ago left, never to return!"

"My exile is over, it is time for me to return. This time I can pay for my passage."

"Nonsenses! I am glad to help a friend in need." The captain responded and the Beyla set sail.

After a month Junichi was back in Japan. The country looked the same to him, no progress nor influence from other countries. Upon his arrival no one recognized him until he arrived to Osaka. The gate guards recognized him, one fell on his knees, bowing and facing the floor, while the other opened the gates announcing his return. Junichi approached one of the soldiers inquiring about the princess.

"The princess is well my lord, but she refuses to talk and never leaves her chamber, she did not mourn her father's passing, she has remained idle for many years now."

Junichi crossed the gate, entered the palace, and all who recognized him bowed at his presence. He finally entered the lightless chamber where Riko sat in a corner, facing silence.

He sat in front of her saying, "My queen I am here." she did not recognize him nor seem to notice a difference. He grasped her shoulders and shook her gently, saying, "Riko do you recognize me?" But she did not move, Junichi looked away for an answer. He had been exiled and had lived for five years thinking she was dead, now that she was alive he was not going to leave her alone, nor give up on her. He gently lifted her chin so to look at her eyes saying, "Riko it is me, your Junichi, the one and only man who has ever loved you." He kissed her.

As if by magic, she embraced him, when she pulled away in tears she replied, "What took you so long?"

"I am sorry Riko, I was busy being your general I forgot to pay attention to my heart." He embraced her and began to cry, "Now that I have laid down my sword, I am open to be the man you love."

It is fair to say, that my friend Junichi lived happily ever after until the end of his days, trading the art of the sword for the art of marriage, protecting Riko, supporting her by helping the people of Japan to enter a new age of progress, and remaining at her side.

CHAPTER XV

おぶ

As for me, some time passed between receiving a letter from Junichi reciting his return journey, twelve months later another regarding the birth of his son, then one day three Danish brothers came to my farm to settle a dispute regarding whom among the three was to marry the princess they saved.

Their story is as followed: When they came of age they each decided to leave their homestead and learn a new craft; Malthe, the eldest, despite his masculinity and popularity with women, traveled to Burgos, Spain to learn the ark of knitting in the Abbey of Santa Maria la Real de las Huelgas. Lars, the middle son was quite the archer, and redefined archery across Europe by going to tournaments, but never used his skills for warfare, despite the fact he opened an archery school and when challenged simply injured his opponents. The youngest son, Villads, went on a separate path, undertaking the skills that define a thief.

Malthe was quiet and reserved; his personality was serious and did not share his experience in the monastery. Lars on the other hand was eager to tell me his story.

"I learned my skills from an Arabic manuscript." He said with a sharp Danish accent, "The best type of shooting is to hold the arrows in the draw hand and not on a quiver so to shoot on a single motion by placing the arrow on the right side of the bow, for a faster reload, this allows speed."

"Tell them about your tournament!" said Villads with the same accent, but his tone was more playful than Lars.

"When I went to London for the grand archery tournament I requested to be the final contestant out of thirty. The rules were simple, each would loose one arrow to the target, the furthest away from the target was eliminated, and each time the target was placed three passes away from its starting position. This was easy until the speed challenge was brought out; here the final ten competitors had the same accuracy. This challenge consisted of shooting five arrows at the target. So not only was accuracy and precision a challenge but the speed as well, here is where I out shot my competitors. One competitor grew angry and when I walked to retrieve my arrows he shot at me while my back was exposed, but I was able to turn around and grab the arrow in midair and shoot it back, inches away from his foot. This enraged him and he shot another arrow at me, this time I was walking forwards and hit his arrow in midair with mine. All gathered around exclaimed but my challenger was not surprised and kept losing arrows at me. I was twenty passes away from him, this time I began to run and shoot his arrows of the air with mine, he was able to release three, before he loosened the fourth arrow I stood in front of him with my bow, and my speed that removed the arrow of his left hand and placed it on my bow. Finally, one of the soldiers approached and apprehended the man and removed him from the competition."

Villads then began to laugh, pulling his head back then said, "Tell us how the poor man died!"

"Villads that is enough!" shouted Malthe in a serious tone. "There is nothing to laugh at a man's death!"

"It is ok brother." Lars turned to face his brother and made a gesture to calm him down then continued, "When I won the prize and mounted my horse to leave, the same man that had challenged me pursued me and tried to shoot me. Despite maneuvering in the streets of London, evading my pursuer, and not engaging in violence, one arrow hit my horse and as I began to fall of the horse, I was able to shoot back but missed him. When I landed, he shot the next arrow I jumped, took the arrow in mid the air and shot it back at him, this time the arrow penetrated his left hand, from the middle knuckle, his palm and all the way to the wrist."

"Please tell us what you told him," Villads began to laugh.

As he did Malthe slapped him saying, "Enough!"

Lars ignored his brothers and concluded saying, "I walked to him and said, 'I am sorry you will never be able to use a bow again but do remember my skills.'"

"I am glad to have such a skilled brother, but now let's tell Yrian the true reason we are here." said Malthe.

"I will be glad to help, but do tell me how you found me," I stated.

"A man named Gerald said you were good at giving advice," the eldest replied.

"Hey, last time you said a Dutch merchant named Theunis said this farmer was an emotional expert!" exclaimed Villads.

"Villads!" Malthe said in a desperate and angry tone. "First of all 'this man,' has a name, and allow me to finish my statements!"

"Please there is no need to be polite, after all I am a simple farmer, but I am flattered to hear that, Villads."

"Do excuse my brother, he is still an impudent child," Malthe said facing his youngest brother, then looked back at me and continued, "Like Villads mentioned, what encouraged me to seek you out was the story captain Theunis shared with me regarding a Japanese samurai."

"Each person is different and has his own story but let me prepare the fire and I will gladly hear all about it," I said.

"It is simple, we rescued a princess, and we can not decide who will marry her!" Villads said in a sarcastic tone.

"Brother, remember we must be fair and consider her thoughts," Lars responded.

I was confused, "Why don't you tell me how you saved the princess?"

"Yes, let us start at the beginning," Malthe finally said. "The three of us reunited after five years of learning our crafts, our father became sick and called us to be with him in his final days."

"Neither of us wanted to inherit his farm and opted to go back to our crafts." Villads added. "However, our mother reveled to us that she was of royal blood and that a cousin of hers had an adopted daughter that was held captive by a warlord. This lightened our eyes and we set out to rescue her!"

"Because it was the right thing to do, save a family relative, not seek out riches and increase the popularity of our names!" Malthe replied.

"Why should I lie?" Villads was fast to reply, in a different tone than before. "Only because I am thief, does not mean I have to steal, I am honest, and I did venture to rescue her so that I was the one to marry her."

"Stop arguing," Lars stepped in. "Malthe promised mother that he would save her, not because he sought fame, but because family was a priority. Villads expressed his sentiment but mother did not find his intentions honorable, so she decided to send the three of us. She asked for my opinion, but I told her that I was going to open an archery school, and did not want her to leave me the farm and the hope of marrying only to settle down. I did however join my brothers to keep them safe from each other, and primarily to provide my skills."

Malthe continued saying, "Our mother's cousin was the wife of a wealthy Jarl in the northern part of Denmark, but one day his village was destroyed by Viking raiders and killed his sons and daughters, leaving no heirs. The raider named Batum the Blind took captive the adopted child named Fjola as a slave. Being that she was loved and cared after and treated the same way as a blood child our aunt begged mother to have one of us rescue her so he might then become high king of Norway."

"Becoming high king of Norway does not sound bad," said Villads as he exhaled.

"Repulsive, how you turned out!" replied Malthe, expressing his distrust for his brother.

"So the three of us set out to find the Viking Batum," Lars continued. "When we reached his village we tried to bargain for Fjola."

"That was my idea," Villads added. "I convinced my brothers by telling them that if we approached Batum by offering a trade, there would be no need to engage in a fight, after all Malthe is no warrior—dedicating his skills in a woman's craft and Lars, despite his skills, was not going to fight an entire army!"

"You and your honeyed words brother, but Batum was not persuaded by your speech craft, the warlord discovered the true identity of Fjola once he intimated you!"

"It was not my fault Malthe, I tried to reason with him, you told him she was a relative when my intention was to anger him so to hear his true motives behind not wanting to give up Fjola, but you had to tell him she was a family relative and then apprehended us, and threw us into a pit, so to feed us to his dragon!"

"It was not a dragon Villads, it was a giant lizard!"

"That is what the 'lizard' is called Malthe," Villads replied using a mocking tone. "The lizard is named Komodo-dragon, or that is what the yellow people of Asia call them."

"When the lizard came out I shot it with my bow the moment it opened its mouth and then I aimed at a hidden archer with a trick shot by curving the flight path of the arrow—instead of flying forwards, the arrow hit the archer behind a barrel."

"Thanks to Lars by shooting five archers in the knees, Batum was shocked when I threatened him saying that he was next!"

Lars then added saying, "Batum was then surrounded by his men, but when I was able to shoot the arrow around the soldier, making their shield useless his men simply ran away."

"I then told Batum that if he did not hand over Fjola, we were going to take his life." Malthe explained. "He instead invited us to dine with him and negotiate in peace."

"I then dismissed myself so to attend private duties," Villads then explicitly expressed how he needed to use the bathroom. "However this was meant as a distraction to set the girl free and take her to a ship, while no one noticed!"

"You then returned and interrupted us when I had the situation under control and asked for a ship instead of the girl, and Batum agreed!"

"Hey calm down! I stole the princess when no one noticed, on a ship that he himself shock my sweaty palm, fair trade, we left on a boat with the girl safely onboard!"

Malthe, the eldest stood up to reply to his brother, "Very clever of you Villads, because it did not take long for Batum to find out!" As a result, Villads stood up, but Malthe continued, "Once we set sail one of his men came out screaming that Fjola, the girl's name by the way, was missing, so Batum with fire arrows burned the sail! If it was not thanks to my 'womanly skills at knitting', he would have killed us right then and there, I repaired the sail, and that is how we got away!"

"In conclusion," Lars stood up, stepped between the two brothers and gently pressed their shoulders, once the three were seated he continued, "We sailed back to Denmark with Fjola, told our story to our mother and she was unable to decide who was the one to marry Fjola."

Villads was about to speak when Lars placed his palm on his mouth and said instead, "She claims that since I saved my brothers from the lizard, and held my peace, I was the one who deserved to marry her, however, Malthe was the one who repaired the ship, and saved us all in the end, and despite Villads profession of choice, she admits that he craftily stole Fjola, and thus deserves a chance to marry her."

"That is why we seek you out good Yrian," Malthe said in his calm voice, "Help us settle our differences and help us tell our mother our intentions."

"Why did Fjola not join the three of you, to seek me out?" I asked.

"She is reluctant to make a choice, I think she is scared that the three of us will turn out the same as other men she has known," Malthe explained.

"Well, her opinion is the one that matters in the end, I would have liked to hear her side of the story, but the solution has presented itself. The three of you, travel back to Batum, and reveal Fjola's true identity, tell him that you will return to the Northern village, it does not matter you tell him who will become jarl of the region, what matters is the truce. Villads, offer Batum your skills, where you can train his men by opening a Thieves Guild, you will be the master. Malthe, tell him that you will provide clothing for his entire village during the winter with warm apparel and the summer with light clothes. Finally, Lars, you can open your school and train both your village and his. "

"How does this help us in marrying Fjola?" Villads asked.

"By each working on your individual trade, and focusing on your personal goals, Fjola will then decide whom to marry. When she chooses either of you, it remains to that brother to romance her."

"I could not agree more," Malthe stood up saying with joy in his voice, then stated, "Like the wise Amelia Barr said, which I will now like to recite to you:

The king may rule o'er land and sea,
The lord may live right royally,
The soldier ride in pomp and pride,
The sailor roam o'er ocean wide;
But this or that, whate'er befall,
The farmer must feed them all.

The writer thinks, the poet sings,
The craftsmen fashion wondrous things,
The doctor heals, the lawyer pleads;
But this or that, whate'er befall,
The farmer must feed them all.

The merchant he may buy and sell,
The teacher do his duty well;
But men may toil through busy days,
Or men may stroll through pleasant ways;
From king to beggar, wate'er befall,
The farmer he must feed them all.

The farmer's trade is one of worth;
He's partner with the sky and earth,
He's partner with the sun and rain,
and no man loses his gain;
and men may rise, or men may fall,
But the farmer he must feed them all.

God bless the man who sows the wheat,
Who finds us milk and fruit and meat;
May his purse be heavy, his heart be light,
His cattle and corn and all go right;
For the farmer he must feed us all.

"Thus, the farmer Yrian has stood out above the bravest warrior in battle that is weary and teary, such is marriage, with a deeper understanding on human empathy, with the determination and jurisdiction of a true king, and keen understanding of human behavior by feeding our hungry hearts, and guided us to remain together as a family, despite our differences! All hail this humble farmer, I bow to you!"

"There is no need for that Malthe," I gently lifted him up.

Lars helped him out, placed a hand on my shoulder and said, "It was never my intent to marry Fjola, but for my part I thank you for giving my brothers, Malthe and Villads, a reason for not fighting, I thank you for giving me an opportunity to remain close with my family."

"You are welcome Lars, just work on sharing your skill, focus on your craft, and do not discard the chance if Fjola chooses you, you are as worthy as any man if any woman approaches to acknowledge your skills."

"By the way brother, I will not be mad if she chooses you, as for me I will enjoy being the leader of Batum's men as the Thieves Guild grandmaster!" Villads hugged me and thanked me.

"That is enough brother, do not startle this poor farmer by picking his pocket while he is unaware." Malthe pulled him aside and hugged me, then said holding my shoulders with his hands saying, "Deep down, all I wanted was to remain close with my family." He then pulled Villads closer saying, "That includes you brother, even if I despise your craft. I do not know whom among us Fjola will choose, nor do I care as long as we remain together as a family!"

They left as Malthe stood in the middle with his arms across both his brothers. The three with their mother and Fjola settled in the North Village and raider attacks became less frequent. This I learned five months later when I received a letter from Fjola reading:

Dear Vrian,

I thank you for helping my brothers in law settle their differences and in a way stop fighting for me as a prize, such men view women as a trophy. When we settled in the village their mother asked whom among the three would become jarl and marry me so to inherit the ownership. Malthe proudly stepped up and said, ` My brothers and I, have decided that Fjola will choose, such is her right as heir to the land. ' Neither approached me to sway my decision, but they were kind to me.

Let me tell you about myself before I tell you whom I married. I grew up as a slave, to a warlord, until a new one killed him and named me their daughter. I never knew my parents, for all I know my mother was a whore and my father a bastard, or so my first master told me, then the man who became my father told me otherwise and provided me the safety of a family. I will ever be grateful for the life he offered me, but deep down, his rules frightened me, I saw family as a new type of slavery.

Malthe, although mature and caring, was going to make me feel as a slave with his love and affection, and I am sure that a woman that values family the same way as he was raised up will truly thank him for his values.

Lars is a skillful man, he can pin a fly to a tree, shoot a bird's nest without harming a single bird or an egg, he is a great warrior, but I do not know his heart, he may protect me, but all he seeks in life is to better himself. He defends our village gallantly, one will argue that if it were not for him, neither of his brothers would have returned with their lives when they faced Batum, but deep down he was protecting their brothers and myself, he did not come to my rescue. He is a great warrior, he keeps us safe and only cares to pass down his skills to other generations, he is a great teacher, but that is not what I, as a woman is looking for.

Last but not least is Villads, he may be a thief, but his view on life is what captivates me, now that I am a free woman I feel this is what I need. He took the initiative to rescue me, he may be selfish, and the act of marrying me may be another way of stealing for him, he may seem as a trickster, but in the month, I saw him from afar, I noticed his determination and his ability to work with others to attain his goals, and I liked that.

Villads did not steal my heart, despite that he was the one who came to my rescue, his motivation to rescue me was to marry me, then I learned how his brothers sought to make a decision, and I do not blame you, I deeply thank you Yrian, for your consideration towards women, the way they worked individually and peacefully without forcing me in the end, is how I was draw by Villads and his motivation all along.

I hope I made the right decision, pray that I can provide him other motivations now that he is a Jarl in Denmark. As a wife I pray one day he will become a loving father. I will like to share with you the poetic side of Villads, the sweet words he told me on our wedding night, I worked them in to this poem:

He ventured far and wide,
with no purpose in mind.
Unquestioned by none
concealing his inner thoughts.
Neither joy, nor aspirations he sought.
Restless and weary,
he did not want to study.

He roamed, saying,
"With this axe I travel alone
The land is vast and I have no home.
Oh, who can tame my wild heart?"

He glanced at a mirage,
yet her visage
did not reply back.

His premeditation
urged him to conquer.
Without his master,
he could not muster
his courage.

In separation
he found despair.
In his hollow thoughts
he heard a song.
The wanderer of this verse,
did not know then
that the song was set
in a distant future.

When the moment came,
and it was her, not him
who professed her love,
it was the same melody
that brought a tear of joy
to the warrior who would return home,
lay down his arms, to open
his arms to embrace her,
the one who questioned
singing a song,

"where can I find
he who would love me
until the end of time?"

No longer in song,
this time the warrior
responded with his own voice,
"look into my eyes
and you will know it is me!"

As a woman I noticed how he disguised his feelings, but when I approached him,
saying, 'who will love me until the end of time', and he replied to me, 'look into my
eyes and you will see', and shared with me how empty he was inside living as a thief,
and as a woman, if I am able to tame his wandering heart, I feel safe.
Good Ynian, may God bless you and preserve you, thank you.
Sincerely, Fjola.

CHAPTER XVI

❧ ☙

The next morning, I saw the red bird. It began to fly around me signaling to follow. I sprinted through the woods following its trail. Thoughts rushed through me about Portia, what will happen if I see her, what will I say? In a glade there she stood. Did I find her, or did she find me? Slowly, I approached her.

"I must be dreaming," I stated in amazement.

"After all this time this is the first thing you say to me Yrian?" She smiled—to me her eyes sparkled brighter than the sun. She took a few steps closer then said, "A doctor's occupation is hard and demanding, but so is love. That which you seek, and I do not know if I can give you what you ask of me, but I am willing to try." There was a long pause, "Why am I saying this, I should be doing my duty."

I did not hesitate and embraced her with all my strength. "Do not say that, I have been longing to see you ever since I last saw you! Portia, I am but a humble farmer but I can love you. You grant me vision so that I can grow and work towards a greater goal! It is hard, but it is not impossible."

"Yrian..." she embraced me again and did not let go of me, "Love is a sickness that which not even the most experienced of doctors can heal, yet it has moved me this far, to seek you out."

Then she met my eyes, "I have to go now, but take what I can give... my emotions. Know that when you see my red bird, I am close to you." She began to walk away but not from my heart, for she was a part of it.

I never imagined this reunion with Portia to be enigmatic, where silence and absence worked together to build up emotion. On my way back to the farm I stopped by the shrine of St. Michael to give thanks for this opportunity.

Through the course of the year I visited Portia in whatever town she was working, once every month, trying to convince her to join me on a trip to Norway to see the Northern Lights, and through persistant convincing she agreed. I learned where her parents lived and I traveled to their homestead and asked her father to accompany me on the journey to Norway on the month of May and he agreed.

I then sought out the closet person I had to a father, John the Miller in the town where I had grown and studied as his apprentice. I was glad to see him active and healthy with a smaller belly, and to my surprise Jack and Jim were working up a sweat, too busy to hear my whereabouts for a change, "Good to see you Yrian, wish you can tell me all about it but I have to deliver this sacks of flour on my fast steed!" said Jim.

"Likewise, I have to use my strong horse to move the merchandise to the new barn, yes things have changed around here," said Jack mounting his horse, galloping to the barn.

"I will be glad to stand at your side on such an important day of your life my boy, besides Jack and Jim will look after the place!" John agreed to travel to Norway.

In April I found a merchant who used to be a Viking named Jorgensen who agreed to take Portia, her parents, John and myself to Tromso. At the end of the month, we set sail to the Northern most part of Europe.

I awoke in frozen tundra, only to see the land of Tromso months after winter, with some snow still on the landscape. I walk out of the boat as a wanderer standing from past to present with empty hands, and little to expect. Coins slip from my sweaty hands, I do not wish to pay the toll of this unbroken road, made out of gravel cement, built on top the ancient stones that serve as the foundation of Norway.

After paying the toll, a cart drives me far up the mountains on the top of the Polar Circle casting my shadow below the lay of the land. Once inside the inn, the bard sings of distant horizons, where the sun shines bright at dawn. In my mind I picture the times of the Norse Saga, under an ancient sun that glitters, melting snow, creating a mirror to gaze into days of old, and trolls roam the land after they had mowed their lawns.

Finally, murky clouds turn to a night without stars. We now wait for the fog to clear the atmosphere. The men order a mug of sweet mead; next we hear a winter's tale, as merchants enter the Bannered Mare—the inn where the town's folk feast in merriment after working in streets of Whiterun. Silence fills the air; the sky gives me an icy sight.

I walk out to cool my thoughts and see the totems, those standing stones that pray to the constellations that sparkle above the midnight sky. I contemplate, wishing to gaze upon the stars before this eve reaches its journey's end. Before the dawn, I may yet see the dancing lights in the Northern sky, creating the stage so I may profess my vow of eternal love.

The calm before the storm beacons a start with a chance meeting. Out of the cold, the gatherings of North Men sing. Portia—the owner of my heart, asks me to join the feast around the fire, while shadow and echoes dance with the flow of the rhythm.

Caught off guard by the feast, a Northern Light, an Aurora has filled the sky with its radiance and dance. All stand still, like blood and steel that drips down from a corpse. The hill shines like towers and shadows. Portia is filed with joy at this spectacle; I have to take seven thousand steps to muster my courage. Solitude will no longer be my companion. As beautiful this sight can be, it has turned to a gathering storm else this moment be gone in an instant.

"This is magnificent. Yrian, I am glad you are here with me," Portia tells me, holding my hand.

So, with the sky above, and my voice within I kneel before her and say, "This night pales in comparison to the sight you give me, nor to the beauty of spending my life next to you." I offer her a ring that looks like a golden tree, and in its branches a shiny stone.

When I hear "Yes" my past and my hardships all culminate to create this moment, and most importantly, my quest has just begun.

"Skol, to this couple!" shouts Jorgensen lifting his cup.

I rise, hugging her, lifting her off the ground and spinning her in the air. When I stop she asks, "What if I had said no?"

"Portia, I waited for the chance to meet you, I waited when you had no time to spare, I waited for you to be ready; I can wait, so you can be with me, but I want only to be at your side for the rest of my life."

"And I am glad to share this night with the most important people in our lives." For the first time she kisses me, and the moment turns to bliss.

"Wind guide you Yrian!" Jorgensen comes and congratulates us. His wife pulls him aside saying, "If only you had the nerve to be this romantic, husband."

"Wife, let me recite to you a love story unmatched by mortals!"

We gathered around the fire to hear the Lay of Jorgensen, based on the Sun Song by Solarlioth:

> Of life and mighty deeds
> that which a warrior strives—
> swearing oaths of fealty
> defending land and king.
>
> Nor health nor wealth—though all go well,
> misfortune of the heart befell
> for the might of love had brought grief,
> my life torn and fair wife left alone in the world!

115

By myself I laid on bloodied field,
as I lay weary and weak of strength
wayfarer I welcome, tis no lack of courage
nor e'er came to my aid, tis death's final decree.

On the following day did a Valkyrie arrive:
"Valhalla awaits ye with rich boon.
Rejoice your ferocious death
as we cross Bifrost to enter Odin's hall!"

The sun I saw: it seemed to me
as on God Almighty I gazed;
lowly before him the last time I bowed,
in this world of living weights.

Oh mighty Father, oh matchless Son,
oh Holy Ghost of Heaven:
hearken to our prayer who hast made us,
to free us all from evil!

Yet my speech escaped from me!
I left behind lands of ridges
and promise of St. Peter's door
all for flight to Odin's hall.

In Asgard I laid eyes on the fallen who said to me:
"Seek ye food, boasting, drinking and song unending?
Welcome where the merriment never ends!"
My sin swelled, I was out of God's grace.

"What brings you, wayfarer grim,
to wander here in Valhalla,
souls-end, Odin's gift to honored dead?"
And there he stood, the one-eyed Aesir.

"I seek the Hall of Virtue!
for no shade am I,
thus I dare enter not into this realm!"
Proudly now did I profess.

My words gave sudden stop to the feast.
With one eye his stare was not grateful,
for who is wise and wary
to challenge that which he does not understand?

"By what right do you refuse my hospitality?"
"Only by righteousness, for I live with virtue,
I speak the truth even if it leads me to a second dead!
I fight to safeguard the helpless, not for glory!"

"Ah, behold a humble soul!
Living or dead, you may pass Bifrost again
'til I judge you worthy by the warrior's test.
Choose your weapon and I will wage your mettle!"

"Oh, Lord of the Aesir,
before we begin, allow me to walk the gardens
so that I may prepare my mind before such a test."
Odin allowed and I went to pray

on a garden of myth and fabled legends
course hauled by hidden path,
from the light would hide, for the Lord to see,
his forgotten son, from his heaven.

I returned to face the battle blinder
Who awaited me holding Gungir,
"Draw thy sword from its scabbard!"
he commanded impatiently.

I lifted my sword hand to reveal flowers.
"What rashly thou wrought'st in anger
now adds more ill to it! Yet by good deed soothe
who grieved you, that they say, is good for the soul.

Humans to God shalt ever
for good things pray,
woefully ill fares every one
who does not find his father.

Above all, beg that boon of him
of which thou know'st most need;
he misses all who asks for naught:
heeds no one the silent one's needs."

The true God then bade the good one's soul
to enter into his bliss;
but the evil foes will not early be
relived from e'erlasting pain till Ragnarok came.

"This was a mighty deed!
The boast of Valhalla
encompassed at last,
by feat of charity none the less.

The Choir of Angels shall sing of your victory!
But your fate lies elsewhere.
When you have completed your count of days,
I may welcome you again,

With glad friendship,
and bid you join my blessed prayer.
When you are ready to join the living,
just bid me so, and I will send you back."

"Not yet Heavenly Father,
allow me one prayer at your side
that I may never tarry from my path,
for you to dwell and lead my actions!"

Prayer behoove to tell my father how happy I was
and prized to have become a man of integrity;
and this also, how the Son of Men
dread to die from this world, for my sins and guilt!

The sun I saw, and so He shone
that bereft of my senses I seemed:
but over against him in Heaven I was not
for now I laid resting mixed with blood.

The sun I saw with trembling sight,
affrighted and fait I was;
for most woefully was my heart
torn in twain, cast onto this world of pain again!

The sun I saw, and since never,
after that dreary battle day;
far away the waters vanished:
cold, I parted from death's care.

From my breast did fly a new breath of life,
and hence, my star of hope,
I now made my way back home
to see my forlorn wife!

"Longer than any lasted this night
when, stiff, I lay on empty bed;
which smoothly shows, as said our Lord,
your husband is made of the mould.

Knoweth, alas! The loving God,
he who made heaven and earth,
unloved how many must leave this world,
thought kith and kin they had."

"Fear not dear wife of mine!
Of his works, every one the reward reapeth:
happy he who does good:
away from pride, I was given a chance at His sight!"

"On the porch sate I nine days;
I fared, without and within;
below and above I sought better ways,
where most easily I could fare."

"Behold this flowers I offer thee,
I bring them from a land of myths!
Rode did I upon Valkyrie wings
crossing Bifrost to the halls of Valhalla!"

"Had holy maidens cleansed the soul of sin!
Thou canst not flowers even from Eden's mist
when here I waited and wept in nightmare dreams,
fearing I may never lay eyes on you eve again!"

"Tardily came I, dear love of mine
to the threshold of our home.
Thither will I, for that was the pledge,
and I now proclaim it again on to thee:

Since long have I sought your sight
in the heavenly skies, longing your company
in countless Aurora glimmering lights
for none to romance me, the way, only you know.

When first I laid eyes upon you,
I visualized in prayer, and made it my quest
that I would marry you
or no woman otherwise!"

"Ye who has encouraged me in my career,
that man, means more to me than any other man,
but among the Trinity, the Choir of Angles and Saints,
there is none, who shape fantasy into a reality, the way you do."

Here my story ends, and so happy ever after, likewise, awaits you.

THE END